I0754120

A

DIPLOMAT'S DIARY

BY

JULIEN GORDON

PHILADELPHIA
J. B. LIPPINCOTT COMPANY
1891

J.B. LIPPINCOTT
STEREOTYPERS AND PRINTERS
COMPANY

A DIPLOMAT'S DIARY

December 30.—Would God I had never seen the Princesse Flavie, or Madame Harnay, that miserable sycophant, as cruel and wicked a counsellor to her royal mistress as she has been a false friend to me and others! Was ever a rat caught in such a hole! What! I am in bad odor at court, and with the Empress; must decamp for the nonce because a silly woman and a base one have . . .

Well, they fancied, did they, that they could so dispose of me, so encompass and trap me? Did they think that because I am a bluff, honest, outspoken sort of fellow, and loyal to my sovereign, I could be taken in such a broken net? There were too many holes in it, mesdames, and you forgot that a grizzled diplomat who has learned the arts of dissembling and of strategy soon recognizes and fathoms such jejune manœuvres.

Gott in Himmel! here I am sent off on this fool's errand in the depth of what promises to be a Siberian winter, so that a broken heart shall have time to mend itself and a ripple of idle gossip to subside. It is too absolutely absurd! What a twinkle there was in the old man's eyes, to be sure, when he bade me farewell! "This mission is a delicate one," he said, "but a man who can extricate himself from the hands of his enemies as you did at S. can beard the Czar in his den, Narishkine et Cie! Only to you would I intrust this secret trust." Beloved old man! He pressed my hand warmly.

"*Va, tu es un brave garçon!*" he said.

"Brave?" Yes, brave, as the world goes here! Brave to prefer my own name and my own laurels, my own modest fortune and self-won honors, to the slavery of a hateful union the titles won by a low compact and the ill-starred gains of a wealth wrung from the foolish affection of an hysteric girl.

Bah! And to say I did hesitate one moment! There is the blemish on my 'scutcheon! The one weakness I blush for to-night under my cap, in the stuffy wagon of this dirty train, which is puffing me away towards the haven where I would not be.

Yes, I was tired. I, strong, self-nurtured, self-reliant I, hesitated a moment. What was it for? The girl? The illustrious connection? The hunting-grounds in the Hartz Mountains? Leisure and indolence? The . . . booty? No! Ten thousand times no!

What was it, then, that made me chicken-hearted for an hour? Tired, old man, tired! I remember that an ancient sage said, "Go not thou to meet thy fate; it is seeking thee," or words to that effect (I was never an apt quoter), and I told myself this was the shibboleth, and that the Princesse Flavie was my fate, and Madame Harnay its messenger. Not an angel one, surely!

Bon! Here we stop; the Russian opposite

snorts as loudly as the engine, and, waking up, asks me to give him a light for his cigarette. I light my own, and I look out through the dim smoke on the little wayside station. People are getting out hurriedly to take a train for Breslau. A splendid couple are walking up and down, both hugely tall and wrapped in furs. The lady has weary blue eyes, which are effective. They are followed by "smart" servants, as the English say. I think they must be themselves English or perhaps Russian. They are unknown to me. The lady is *chic* in a big, grand way; not like a Parisian. The man looks like an officer.

There! they have vanished into the waiting-room, and I shall see them no more forever. My neighbor, the Russian, wishes to talk. My thoughts not being agreeable, I am not averse to listening. He tells me his name is Paul Pantchoulitzew. He gives me his card, and I find he is a *gentilhomme de la chambre de S. M. l'Empereur de Russie*, a title somewhat vague, and which, I believe, is conferred on nobody in particular for no particular motive.

He looks like my brother Marc. He is rather an elegant fellow, which goes without saying, as he resembles a member of my family.

Well, "Marc" tells me he is forty, and is going to Riga to be married. I do not tell him that I am forty-two, and am going to Petersburg to avoid marriage. It would sound flat.

I covertly observe him, and catch a crooked reflection of myself in a cracked mirror opposite. The comparison favors me. I look younger than he. Yes, there is no doubt of it. This is a consolation for all the vexations of the past, and the indignation that chokes me when I think that I am to be doomed to pass the next six months in a country I abhor. It is something to look younger than one really is, and is as pleasing to Antony as it would be to Cleopatra, for, look at it as boldly as we will, face it as courageously as we may, age is tragic. It means "get out of the way!" *Faites place aux jeunes.* It means the retired list, respectability and inanition.

I wonder if it was the first signs of decadence that made me hesitate a moment when the Princesse's hand was offered to me! Probably. It is an agreeable fact to remember, however, that I could not, when I was a boy officer of twenty, have repudiated the thought with hotter violence, and that the lassitude of will came after maturer consideration. The fires, it seems, still smoulder. I sigh, and ask myself to what purpose.

December 31.—Here we are at the Russian frontier! We are at once pounced upon by a set of barbarians. Queer-looking guards, in wide light clothes, with pompons on their heads, surround us. They want our passports. I hail Gustav, who emerges with dishevelled hair and limp uniform, his nose redder and crookeder than usual. Gustav says his nose was peppered with shot in the war, but if its symmetry was marred in the conflicts of battle or of love, certainly it is not ornamental.

I am cross, and find fault with him; and he searches wildly for my passport in the depths of a mysterious valise from which he never parts for an instant. He mutters that that idiot August must have made away with it. Here August, my orderly, appears on the scene, *frais et dispos*, with his curled blonde moustache, and his white hands. He finds the passport, with indignant *sang-froid*, on the top of my dressing-case, and scorns to answer Gustav's sneers. All the time he is smiling at the slender maiden who is peddling nothing less innocent than *chay* and little cakes, and making eyes at my pretty man-servant. She evidently looks upon me and "Marc" as upon excellent, respectable, middle-aged men of doubtful charm. Ah, youth! Youth, beautiful, inconstant: how soon thou spreadest thy wings!

Strange, that vanity, which Flavie's passion for me might have roused in a less philosophical mind, has not been awakened within me! No, not a breath!

My papers require only a glance. My personal recommendation to His Majesty from His Majesty lay me open to much boot-licking and obsequious courtesy. My boxes are hardly unlocked, while the other passengers wring their hands and cry in vain over their emptied trunks, duly rummaged by official fingers.

A lady in a long *café au lait* cloak, lined with white fur, and with a white fur cap on her blonde red hair, has just walked through the station. She is rather a picturesque figure, albeit her costume is too showy. How few women have attractive backs! There is an eloquence in a woman's back. This woman's shoulders are not satisfying; they are artificial. I remember the back of a certain Greek goddess in the Hermitage Sculpture Galleries. It is several years since I saw it during that hurried passage through Petersburg on my way to Bucharest, and yet I recall distinctly its strong and reposeful beauty. I must go and have another look at it some afternoon, when I can rest an hour from my cares of state. Thank God I have the knack of speed, and in the afternoons I shall have time to study art.

I remember how happy I was in Venice

seven years ago, how I revelled in its glories. Men, intrigues, political and social, the arts of war and of government, personal ambitions, all fell from me, and even you, mesdames, had no share or parcel in my reveries. I would like to die in Venice! A woman would have spoilt it all. They always do! And now . . . to sleep.

January 1.—I look out upon the stretches of lonely steppes. Not the real steppes, they tell me, but they are real enough for the foreigner. It is cold, and I light my cigarette, and puff smoke against the window, that the warmth may loosen the light film of frost upon the pane. So . . . I gaze upon a dim white world. Here and there low-lying hamlets, huts huddled together pathetically in the grayness of the early dawn, as if for mutual support and warmth, their tan-colored roofs the one bit of color against the sombre sky. Rarely, very rarely, sledges drawn by horses, some driven by moujiks, and others by their women, move slowly across the waste. The men wear sheepskin coats girt in about their sturdy waists, and boots made of the same hardy material. The women are sexless bundles, dressed like the men, only wearing dingy kerchiefs instead of sheepskin caps upon their uncombed hair. They all look stolid and stupid, but kindly, when they are near enough to the track upon which we stand for us to catch a sight of their upturned faces.

Monsieur Pantchoulitzew, or "Marc," as I call him, does not care to look out. He has kept on his sleeping-cap, and seems restless. He looks at his watch and says "*Katori-chas?*" to the conductor, and finds we are behind time. Evidently he is, or thinks himself, in love. He shows me a photograph of his *fiancée*. She looks like some one—wait! Yes, it is like little Jeanne Overbeck. How odd in this world that every one reminds us of somebody else!

I once read an essay, by an American philosopher, I think, translated in one of our periodicals; it deplored this fact that everything and every one reminded us of something else. The author thought this most undesirable.

He advocated self-reliance, and the avoiding of imitation. He said we were nowadays only parlor soldiers. I don't know much else of this author, but one sentence clings to my remembrance: it was about "the magnetism of originality." "Even impure and trivial actions are illumined by this science-baffling star, if the least mark of independence appears."

I hate all the Americans I ever have met, but this man certainly had some ideas. To be sure I have only seen a few American demoiselles and their colorless mothers at Baden, Hombourg, and Spa. The girls were not colorless, but something like pretty, scentless flowers, and lacking the *ewige weiblichkeit.* The husbands and fathers were always in America, just embarked or embarking. I fancy that they are better than their women, if they had only the time to be known. The United States is a curious phenomenon, with which they have had something to do.

Well, such as she is, this round-faced Riga young lady who is to marry Mr. Pantchoulitzew seems to be all perfect in his eyes. He is childishly desirous that I shall ask him questions. I ask him a few, because I am good-natured, and so, with the talk, and *chay*, and beer, and cigars, the day slips into the great darkness, and engulfs us at the station of our journey's end. *Petierbourk! Petierbourk! Petierbourk!*

I find myself almost clasped in the arms of Berg, who has everything ready for me. He has the ambassador's sleigh. Ossip, the chasseur, alert and pompous, takes possession of my servants and my valises. Berg pulls me this way and that. We jump into the fur-lined vehicle; Ivan, the coachman, grins; his beard is all covered with silver frost-drops. The little black horses neigh and fret, with a halo of snow on their flowing northern manes. We draw up the great soft skins about our chins, and off we dart like gnomes of the night, quick as a whirlwind through the silent streets.

January 4.—Count Berg has certainly done well for me. I have a large, cheery apartment on the *Quai de la Cour*, close to our embassy, and there is a private stable near where he has four fine horses for me, and a well-appointed turnout. Gustav and August have unpacked my effects. I have been superintending the arrangement of some photographs, books, and *bibelots.*

After breakfast I had a long, earnest interview with Narishkine. He is very cordial, polished, and non-committal. Truly an agreeable man, and a valuable servant to his country, and there is unrolled before me such a vista of possibilities!

This record, however, of my daily life is not to be the confidant of state secrets. I might fall dead of *ennui* one of these cold mornings, and the public censors might pay my domicile an inspectory call, or the secret police invade its sanctities, merely by way of seeing if I leave any last messages for them. No, only my own brain and heart shall be repositories of my sovereign's commands, and of my own tactics in carrying them out.

I will only jot down here and there superficially such light details as may refresh my memory for days and times and people and places.

I am surprised and a little annoyed to find I am to be lionized. I had hoped to arrive unnoticed, and escape all but the necessary visits of ceremony. It seems not. My table is already piled high with invitations. My duty lies largely in courtesy, and I must, with many a grimace, bow to my fate. Lord Faville is here, and it seems he and I are the rivals of the hour. To be coupled with Lord Faville for the favors of fashion! I confess that its whims are not flattering. He is here for pleasure, and I for work.

January 5.—I went to-day at eleven o'clock to wait upon the Czar at the Anitchkoff. It is greatly improved, inside and out, since its erection by the great Catherine. A handsome palace, magnificently furnished; and the private apartments have a cosey modern comfort, with cheerful windows looking on the great "Prospect" and inner courts.

The Czar pressed my hand warmly, and

talked on general topics. It is evident he desires to gain time. He asked elaborately about the health of the royal family, and about my own. He said the Empress would receive me in the afternoon, and dismissed me with an "*Adieu, mon cher!*"—We shall see.

In the afternoon, *en route* to my interview with the Empress, I left my card at all the embassies and legations. Berg accompanied me. He told me the news, the gossip, and the scandals of this naughty town. He told me I must go to the circus on Saturday nights. There was a benefit to the Cornalba on Sunday, which would be fashionably attended by the court, and altogether desirable. There was an exceptionally fine troop at the Marien-sky; and on Mondays I must have a *fauteuil* at "The Italiens." Then, of course, I must officially attend the first ball at the Winter Palace, and a bal-masqué at the Princesse Soltikoff's; and then there were the state dinners to which I had been or would be bidden.

While he talked I looked at him. He is unchanged, except that his hair is grown gray;

much more so than mine, which is hardly tinged at all. He wears it short, and it stands up like a brush on his round head. Berg can hardly be much over thirty-five. He has the same expression as of old, at once *rusé* and ingenuous. In his fur coat and sealskin cap he looks like a young Jesuit priest; in his sword, spurs, and casque, like a rakish soldier.

Berg is deep. I am attached to him in a way, but I do not altogether trust him. He has too much curiosity and not enough imagination to be a comrade to my taste. Still, he knows his place and keeps it.

The Empress looked at me with sweet, cold eyes. She tried, evidently, not to be perfunctory, and I tried not to let her see that I thought her so. In the effort I felt perhaps she might say of me as my Emperor once did of a youthful *attaché* presented to him for the first time. "He treated me with great indulgence."

In her low, slightly husky tones, she said some kind words of flattery, congratulating me on the faith I inspired in my sovereign, and that a man as young as I was honored in being intrusted with such important matters; "for," she added, "I do not meddle in politics, as you know, but I keep still in the current."

This imperial lady dislikes me, I believe, for she hates my nation, and in me she sees to-day an enemy. Ah, my fair foe, I will wage no war on you and yours if you will but smile upon me! I have seen War close; the God of battles has breathed into my ear, and the word he uttered was,—Peace! I kissed her fingers "indulgently," and Berg and I were ushered out by Prince D. and passed down from hand to hand until the sentries saluted us at the palace portals.

Here we met Strogonoff, and stopped to chat with him. I then dismissed my sleigh, and walked home alone. Certainly in the twilight hour this city of pink plaster assumes a fantastic loveliness. I strolled down the Nevsky Prospect with its *va et vient* of rushing *canies*, its crowded thoroughfare of quaint promenaders, a motley crowd of curious folk, hurrying hither and thither like the unreal phantoms of dreamland. Turks, Armenians, eagle-eyed

Jewish pedlers, Russian generals, half hidden in their shubas, fish-venders in their low sledges, offering their unattractive frozen fish, while the pigeons circle about with rustle and flutter and gurgle, trying to get a crumb to stop their hunger pangs.

Opposite the chapel of the Gostinii Dvor, where the little sisters pray night and day, and where the swinging lamps burn before the sacred Icons, a funeral train was passing. To my Protestant simplicity there is much that is repellent in the ceremonial of this half-pagan cult; yet the love of art and the sensuous temperament, which I draw from my mother's family, are, in spite of myself, more or less enthralled by its imposing grandeur. First came fifteen *avant coureurs*, bearing fifteen white satin cushions, on which reposed the decorations of the defunct official. The car was all ablaze with gilded ornament, and drawn by four black horses richly caparisoned. The priest followed, with flowing hair and beard, and then the widow, dragging her sable garments through the snow, alone and unsupported. At a respectful distance from her solitary woe a train of relatives and friends, all afoot.

With the ponderous movement of the Greek ritual it takes half of the day to marry, bury, or baptize. Delicate women stand and walk in the cold for hours, and such is their faith that they faint not. Certainly what we have gained in light we have lost in fervor.

I shall become a "dome maniac" here. These fairy constructions, bubbles of gold blown against the wintry sky, are strangely alluring. I walked through St. Isaac's reverently enough; there was a service of song in progress. It was penetrating in the extreme, and I sighed, with a vain longing, for a breath of my old romance. I looked behind the columns in vain for some fair form which would awaken me to a thrill of joy, or of ardor, but I only saw General Karazin, mumbling his prayers before a battered image. What endless orisons the old reprobate must recite if he means to atone for his merry past!

Ah, romance! delight! how long since I have felt their summons, and how rarely come to us these radiant guests we each of us expect!

White and still seemed the misty quays as I emerged upon them, after the busy Nevsky and the dark cathedral. I lounged along, looking down upon the squalid Esquimaux tents on the Neva, and up at the women of fashion, who smiled at me as they passed like the wind in their luxurious sleighs.

The Princesse Soltikoff stopped to speak, on her way to Madame de Walkenstein's reception. She insisted I must not fail at her masquerade ball the 22d. "You must come *en bourgeois*," she said, "for only the women will mask."

"They always do," I replied.

"And you?" she laughed. "Do you emulate them in this? They call you the impregnable, but I call you the impenetrable. Oh, we have heard. . . . !" and she made a wave of her hand as if encircling wide horizons.

And now to dinner at my embassy; but while I dress I reflect that at forty-two distrust and disillusion have made havoc of a man's fatuity. In the smiles of these dames I only suspect a trap.

January 18.—To-day is the great national festival, "The Blessing of the Waters." It is a pretty, childish whim. I was with the royalties all of the day. I have lived in courts much of my life, yet I am no real courtier. My tastes are simple; I prefer the tent. Personally I am *enragé* for war,—and I have come hither to discuss . . . a peace policy. Personally I love the camp, the bivouac, or, at worst, my quiet rooms, my books, and my pipe, and I am forced to smile and fawn, ground in the mortar of that exacting mistress, etiquette; I am obliged to play the gallant and the courtier.

Why do I do it? why? why? First, because I adore my country, and can so passionately best serve her, and secondly, because I am ambitious, and fame lies here.

This *fête* day is full of color. Travellers should see Petersburg in winter. The streets are filled with merry-makers, merry as these Russian giants can be, with a tinge of *tristesse* always; a sort of half-sad patience. Here and there groups of the disaffected, wild-haired Nihilists, as they are called, gather sombrely. Why are communism and dirt synonymous? The Russian plotters seem to have taken a vow never to clean their nails and heads.

I thought the Empress looked a trifle pale. The *corps des pages* drove up in the gay Imperial equipages. Every grade of the *Tchin* was agog and out in its carriage, and even the sun was brighter than usual for this benediction of the sleeping river. They break the ice to bless the shadowy waters.

In the evening I was invited to a supper given at his rooms by one of the young Chevalier guardsmen, Baron Strogonoff. He is distantly related to the Scheremetiefs, a dashing young fellow, and a favorite at the court. He is said to be deeply in debt, but lives well . . . for that reason. We were fifteen in all. We had a jolly enough time from twelve to one, with songs, stories, and excellent wines, and my own spirits were of the gayest. I was rather surprised when Berg suddenly told me that a lady was expected. She arrived about 1.30 o'clock. It was none other than Madame Nathalie. She came direct from the ballet, and had not waited to . . . dress; the display of her charms was extremely generous.

I regret to say that these young officers had drunk a good deal, and that their manners at this hour were not marked by the self-control and calmness our civilization exacts. The fun had waxed a little loud. Madame Nathalie got more admiration this time than even she had calculated upon; she grew hotly indignant, and a half-hour after her *entrée* draped herself in her shuba and left abruptly. I offered her my arm to her carriage.

"*Ce sont de grossiers animaux, monsieur,*" she said to me. "*Mais vous, vous êtes un grand seigneur.*"

She looked at me boldly with her coarse, soft eyes, but she was a woman after all, and I noticed that her mouth trembled.

"I was one of them, madame," I said, "with them, and in their company, in their name, therefore, albeit a foreigner, I beg your pardon."

She smiled faintly, grasped my hand warmly, and drove away. I should hardly have noted here this trivial incident had it not had a sequel. I found more or less of a brawl when I returned to Strogonoff's dining-room. He had hurried down-stairs only in time to see Nathalie's brougham turning the corner. He was worried and angry, and accused one of his guests, a foolish boy, d'Aubilly, a French *attaché*, of having insulted the danseuse. D'Aubilly protested in half-tipsy deprecation. As for me, decidedly I am losing my taste for such amusements as these, and during the high words which ensued I made my escape unnoticed.

The night was bitterly cold. Under its silent influences my high spirits of an hour before fell. The stories we had told and listened to seemed vapid and witless, the songs ribald and senseless, and the rudeness to the woman vulgar. The fumes of the wine I had drunk had made a fever in my veins, but no exhilaration in my brain. I thought with disgust of the childish freaks of men, and the idiocies and indecencies of it all. I must confess I am not usually given to analysis, although my career might have led me into overmuch finessing. I generally take myself and others simply enough; for unless one does this there can be no action, and I like action, blood, and stir. Simplicity has always seemed to me one idea of genius.

Nathalie's farewell grasp had not been simple to me. It was alluring, inasmuch as nature is always so, and it had been grateful and true, even in the *mima;* yet it was repellent, because her fingers had lingered as much as if to tell me, "We shall see, we shall meet!" Frankly, I have seen all I want of Madame Nathalie; she could only lose on a closer inspection. At any rate, I believe I behaved like a gentleman.

When I got home I bathed my room in the cold moonlit waves of wind, and dismissed all further remembrance of my evening. Gustav came by and by and threw my cloak about me as I sat at the piano, trying to find the key of a refrain I had once heard,—"*Perdus tous deux dans la steppe infinie!*" I sang it over and over, first in this key and then in that,—"*Perdus tous deux dans la steppe infinie.*"

I thought of poor dead Marie, and the empty years since,—empty of heart . . . I forgot that she had been weak, and had renounced me, only to remember that she had once been tender. But somehow the refrain was not made for her: I could not imagine myself happy alone on the steppe with Marie, and an unfelt, unknown premonition stirred within me. Tall and tranquil, this new vision beckoned to me across the night; and here there was no weakness, but only strength and power.

Smoking a cigarette, and still humming to myself, I divested myself of my panoply of war and sought my bed. I had a dream of battle, not of love: I lay wrapped in my cloak by a camp-fire on the hill which overlooked Plevna. I was talking to Stronkoff, of the long golden moustaches, and to

Genghis. Levitzky, too, was there, and we all spoke in whispers of Skobeleff, who was away off fighting on the other side of the hill. We could see the smoke on the distant horizon. It was stormy, and we were cold and wet. A train of wagons came in sight; we knew it was the Grand Duke's commissariat. "I am only an on-looker at this war," I said, and when their big brass samovars were brought I would not touch their hot tea. Then suddenly a man from among the others turned upon me and called me a traitor. I in vain explained to him that I was there through his Emperor's courtesy, and that I bore his people no ill will.

"You see that smoke rising near the redoubt," he said. "Skobeleff's position will be lost through your treachery. Our dead are many, and curse you!"

"Skobeleff," I cried, "is the worst *canaille* that ever shouldered musket or brandished sabre!"

Then they all fell upon me. I turned to grapple with them and defend myself, and awoke suddenly to find that I was wrestling with Gustav.

"The Herr Graff has the nightmare," he said. "*Na, gnädige Herr;* these supper-parties are evil things."

My only satisfaction was that I had expressed my opinion of their general before I awoke. It would have been indiscreet afterwards. I slept, and dreamed no more.

January 19.—After an hour's conference of some importance with a Russian officer upon military matters, I was at breakfast, with my mouth full of *compote,* when the door which leads from my study to my modest dining-room was violently thrown open, and, announcing "a lady desires to see monsieur," August, with a twirl of his curly moustache, ushered in . . . a woman. I had no time to rebuke him angrily at this unlooked-for invasion, when Madame Nathalie swept into my presence. She threw herself breathlessly into a chair, while I wiped my lips with the napkin I still flourished in my hand.

"Have you heard," she cried, clasping her

hands together dramatically,—"have you heard there will be a duel?"

I shook my head, and she went on,—

"It is all the fault of that foolish boy. He has pursued me for many weeks; but even if he had not insulted me, as he did last night, I can confide to you that there was no hope for him, not a vestige!" Here she smiled. "The only man who would have dared to marry me was shot by a Frenchman, and I made a vow I would never give myself to one of that hateful nation! But, after all, this one—he is only *un enfant*, and Strogonoff is a great swordsman. The boy is dead if they fight with swords!"

She spoke hurriedly and excitedly, but a genuine anxiety pierced through the rapture of the *comédienne*, whose vanity was caressed, and of the woman of business, who scented a good advertisement.

Having disposed of my napkin and my *compote*, I asked her, standing up against the mantel-piece, in what way I might serve her,—if perhaps she would honor me by sharing my repast that we might talk over the affair more at leisure?

She freed herself with a rapid gesture from her encumbering furs, and, tossing off the little sealskin cap which rested on her short black hair, she seated herself opposite me at the table, drawing off her long tan gloves.

"What have you got to eat?" she asked, looking at me with her big eyes, through their thick lashes. "How nicely arranged you are, and how pleasantly for a chat! Seriously, *mon cher*, you must stop all this."

Considering that we were to talk over an affair of life or death, I could not, in parenthesis, but admire the excellent appetite and astonishing rapidity with which my fair visitor, as she talked, disposed of pickled salmon, omelet *aux truffes*, mushrooms on toast, and mutton cutlets, with two bumpers of beer, a glass of Vodka, coffee, and a *chasse*.

"I came," she said, showing her white, regular, cruel little teeth, over which her thin lips never entirely close, "because you are a man of the world and, as I told you last night, a *grand seigneur*. No Frenchman would ever have behaved as you did last evening."

"I am so surprised, madame, to hear you speak disparagingly of a great people, which I believed to be your own. Are you not a Parisian?"

"I never could discover," she replied, evidently pleased, "to what nation I did belong, and it has its advantages. I can *faire de la politique*, with impartiality. Mamma said she was a . . . Styrian, and about papa," she added, laughing, "there always seemed to be some doubt. *À propos* of the French . . . last night, do you know, I began to adore their enemies."

I bowed, but these unsought confessions were becoming intensely disagreeable to me. Madame Nathalie, I had to admit to myself, looked far more attractive in her simple dark cloth costume, which fitted to perfection, and threw out into bold relief, while somewhat subduing, the magnificent proportions of her bust and hips, than she had in her tulle and tinsel. She had used cosmetics very sparingly this morning, and in all her poses there was the strength of the gymnast in repose.

I realized that these splendid feminine charms, to which were added the gestures and facial expressions of a debased gamin, might have for many men great piquancy.

She leaned her face upon her hands, which were boneless and soft, the hands of the woman of pleasure. She looked across the table at me.

"Yes, they say the women of the world like to be treated *à la légère*, but we . . . artists"—she hesitated a moment to find a correct word—"we . . . artists appreciate a distinguished man who understands us and treats us with respect."

"And about this duel?" I said, impatiently, pretending not to notice her challenging glances. There was something magnetic to me in the woman's regard; but the pole of repulsion was there. I was a man, and her evident admiration of my humble person stirred within me a certain brutal satisfaction, but I wished at all hazards to be rid of her, and of a folly which might prove troublesome and even contagious, like some undesirable malady.

"Ah, yes!—the duel! I was saying—what was I saying?" and she laughed. I can imagine nothing less pleasant than Nathalie's laughter.

"You were saying," I said, sternly, "that young d'Aubilly was a doomed man if it took place, and that there had better be no delay. I will go at once to his ambassador's and see what can be done to stop the nonsense. The boy was tipsy, and you surely cannot wish him punished. And then," I added, more gallantly, "it was, after all, your own fault. He is not the first whose blood you have fired." I rose and began to buckle on my sword.

"Would you leave me like this?" she said, plaintively. "Don't you ask me to . . . come again? How strong you are, and robust!" she added, watching my every movement, as if fascinated.

"I am very strong, madame," I replied, "but there are some tests to which I should not dare to put myself." And getting my casquette down from its peg, I almost pushed past her to the door.

I could see she was intensely piqued. She was putting on her hat half-way on the stairs.

"I will stay longer next time," she cried over her shoulder at me defiantly, with a saucy shake of her black mane.

When the door had closed upon her, I went back, stepped into my bedroom, and buried my face in a great basin full of fresh cold water. I then washed my hands and polished my nails elaborately, poured out a glass of Tsarskoe Selo water from its brown *cruche*, and quaffed it with avidity. She had left a queer smell of chypre behind her, which I detested.

"Go out, August," I called, "and get some flowers for the vases in my study, and let them be such as have a strong perfume."

August grinned. He evidently thought me a lucky fellow for a man of my years. In the street I met Berg, who told me the challenge had been exchanged, but the French ambassador had stepped in, and an apology would be made.

"Fancy," he said, "fighting for that *canaille*, but by Gad, she is a superb creature *au physique*. Why, Strogonoff is mad after her. You ought to cultivate her, if you want to find out things; they say she knows no end of state secrets."

"I will choose some less-expensive methods of information," I said, laughing, while we clanked along arm in arm, exchanging salutes with many acquaintances. "Avoid women scrapes," was my last bit of home advice.

"*Tiens!* did they think it necessary? I thought you were called the impregnable," chuckled Berg. "That is the name with which they dub you here. Your reputation has heralded you."

I changed the subject. Berg grows familiar. We hailed a passing *çani*, and drove off furiously, crossing the Fontanka Canal, with its great granite walls. All the world was in the street. The Russian *isvoztchik* is certainly very picturesque, with his long blue coat, wide girth, and low-crowned hat, which looks like those queer velvet pin-cushions one sees at charitable fairs.

We passed the American minister's sleigh with its black Orloff trotters, blue cloth reins, fat coachman, bearskins, and chasseur,—quite a good equipage. There was a lady with the *Poslonniek*, middle-aged, probably his wife. Now I remember these people receive to-morrow, and I must pay my respects.

Visits of ceremony to uninteresting people are the thorn of my profession. I am told these Americans are very respectable, correct, and well-bred people. I take little interest, however, in the nation they represent; their traditions are *nil*, and their institutions intensely antipathetic to me. They are a remarkable people, but they have no sympathy. I have never had any curiosity to see them at close quarters, and shall probably avoid visiting them in their own country. However, I will go into their legation for fifteen minutes to-morrow. Civility costs little. I am wrong: civilities seem to cost a good deal sometimes.

My own to Madame Nathalie, for instance, if she be true to her sex, will bear fruit, at any rate.

I shall not be the mere caprice of a depraved woman, for now I have touched her imagination. If I know anything of her captious sex, Madame Nathalie is thinking of me at this very moment, and is plotting my downfall. Ha, ha, ha! Her lovers, who will shower her to-night with jewels and with flowers, at her benefit, will be, with their gifts, as dross in her eyes. Make place for me, messieurs, at least for a few hours! I am the unattainable. Ah! if men only knew—and women too!

I stop at some of the brilliantly-lighted French jewelry shops on the Nevsky and buy a few trinkets to send home. I choose a quaint jewelled book-mark for the Princesse. She cannot wear it, and it is much better. Only a woman I love shall ever wear aught that I have given to her! I have promised to be a friend to that lonely girl, and if that devil, Harnay, does not again work on her *exalté* temperament by drawing exaggerated pictures of my supposed concealed attachment, I will be the best friend and support she ever has had. With a frivolous, unkind father, utterly regardless of her, and with no mother or sister upon whom she can lean, she is indeed to be pitied.

All that episode is full of vexation. To think that a few dances at the old schloss, a few games, a little kindness, should have been so misinterpreted! I am one of the least vain of men, yet here——!

January 20.—I had a long seance with Narishkine this morning. Like Caprara, he kept on his glasses, that I might not see his eyes. As ever, he was supple and eluding,—but all serious matters in connection with my mission I note not here.

My morning has been entirely eclipsed, I admit, and overshadowed by my afternoon. The morning was earnest, arduous, difficult. The afternoon has left with me a sense of pleasure, and an aroma delicate and subtile, like the taste of some rare wines. I smile in writing it down. It all came from an hour I passed with the Americans. Having left cards on one or two ladies, who were not at home, I had myself carried to 81 Sergievskaya. The United States minister, like most of his compatriots, is rich, and lives well. They have hired Count de Vlassow's little palace, which they have furnished and arranged with considerable elegance. When ushered in I found Madame North surrounded by a number of callers. She was doing the honors of her salon with affability and simplicity. After engaging her in conversation for a few moments, I wandered across the room to the tea-table, where I soon found myself wedged in behind the samovar, between Lady Xavier and her daughter.

The latter was attired in a green gown, with some red about it here and there, which exactly matched her hair and eyebrows, and of which the effect was painful. The tea-table stands under some large palms at one end of the drawing-room, and about it the younger people seem to cluster, while Madame North detains the older ones nearer the door, where she receives. The room is cheery and home-like, with deep low lounges, a few fine pictures, an *encombrement* of bric-à-brac disposed on their *étagères* and tables, shaded lamps, and a bright wood fire. The heated walls of Russian houses make them intolerably warm. Buttoned closely up in our uniforms, how we poor officers do suffer! These rooms were cooler than is usual, and their atmosphere was extremely agreeable.

Well, as I say, I was exchanging inanities with Miss Xavier, who is not my affinity, and whose hair was redder and whose cheeks were larger than usual, and was meditating a speedy escape, when there was a slight stir at the door. At the same moment Lady Xavier tapped me on the shoulder with her long gold eye-glass.

"Who is the distinguished-looking woman in violet velvet?" she asked, in a sharp whisper.

Detaching herself from the group with whom she had entered, and distinct from them all through some intangible unresemblance, the person in question came forward, with a slightly *trainant* movement, towards the table where we sat. Seeing that we were all unknown to her, and that we were at the same time watching her she half stopped, irresolute for a moment, and looked back a little appealingly at the lady of the house. Mrs. North came out quickly from among her friends, and, putting one arm lightly about the younger woman's figure, propelled her gently in our direction. I rose.

"Lady Xavier, let me present to you my niece. My niece—Miss Xavier. Monsieur, may I present you to my niece?"

The name was mentioned twice, but these foreign syllables stick in the teeth of their utterer, and I am not quick at unravelling their mysteries. I found myself standing rather awkwardly in front of the "distinguished lady in violet velvet."

She bowed to me vaguely, not looking at me particularly, and sank into an arm-chair close to Lady Xavier's elbow.

"I am tired," she said.

"Have you been sight-seeing, my dear?" asked Lady Xavier, in that patronizing tone in which older important women address young insignificant ones. I could see she was thoroughly "taking in" the elegant figure of the new arrival. I was already wondering how many days it would take for her persistent malevolence to awaken and sling its envenomed arrows at this new and inviting target. I had known Lady Xavier many years, and had followed her through various vicissitudes of far less splendid days. I knew her foibles.

"Yes, a little. I did some of the churches. My uncle took me out."

"You have only just arrived?" asked Gladys Xavier.

Let me see. Yes, it is not a week yet. It seems years;" and she sighed.

"Why, don't you like Petersburg?" said Miss Xavier, with round eyes.

"My daughter enjoys every minute here; there is a great deal of fun for the younger people," said the mother.

"After the court balls commence, and you have been presented, you will enjoy yourself immensely. You can skate at the Tauride, and all that," said Gladys.

"Oh, balls? I have been to so many balls," said the violet lady, evidently not impressed.

By the way, it was a charming toilet. She had left her wraps in the hall, and wore a closely-fitting pansy-colored gown, which draped her shapely slenderness to perfection. I don't know much about the detail of a woman's costume, but this was certainly very harmonious. It fell in a straight fine line to her feet, and there was gleaming black jet about it. On her head she wore a very becoming toque of the same sombre hues. She had a thin white veil tightly drawn across her face, but it did not reach her mouth. It was the flower-like mouth of a girl of twenty. The veiled eyes were wiser.

She leaned far back in the low causeuse, but there was a suspicion of daring in her abandon. Lavater infers character from gait and attitude: under this woman's tranquillity there evidently lurked a plenitude of force and of energy. The wild creatures of the woods and of the deserts have this repose when at rest.

As she had not deigned to notice me, I had plenty of leisure for surmises. Lady Xavier studied her too. I fancied she was already beginning to disapprove.

Old Prince Bodisko was talking about Madame Skobeleff *mère* to some young ladies near the tea-table. He talked loudly, and all turned to listen.

"I knew her," he said, "a handsome, clever woman. She came to Petersburg with her pretty daughters, full of projects, of ambitions; but we are not amiable here, and they were not received. The Countess X., who made the sunshine and the rain for us then, was giving a ball. She was asked an invitation for the Skobeleff ladies. 'What! invite that *canaille* to my house?' she asked. The cruel reply was brought to Madame S. 'Did she say that?' asked the mother. 'Her son shall marry my daughter!' And," added the prince, "he did."

"And he has paid well since for his mother's affront to his mother-in-law," said a young woman, amid quickly-quelled laughter.

The lady in violet had listened intently to

Bodisko's anecdote, and I noticed that a slight flush rose in her cheeks, and into her eyes a look of triumph.

"That was well done," laughed the others.

"My dear, let me present you to the Countess Barythine," said Mrs. North, addressing her niece.

The old Countess, such a well-known figure in St. Petersburg society that description is superfluous, glided forward with extended fingers. She wore her richest sables and her suavest manners.

"Charmed," she said, "to make your ac quaintance;" and, after a few commonplaces, "When you get bored in the gay whirl," she said, "you can come and sit with me now and then. I love young people. I will present you to my niece Wasia. Wasia is very pretty and *à la mode*. You will see her at court. She will wear a lovely wreath of white chrysanthemums with one of the big Oblensky diamonds in the centre of each. They were her mother's. It is a great risk, but young women nowadays don't value heirlooms. She has just shown me the wreath. I shall not go to the ball: I have nothing to wear; I am greatly impoverished. The expenditure for my good husband's mausoleum, with the depression of the ruble, has swallowed up half of my fortune. I only hope his family appreciate what I have done for his memory. Since his death I have lived in retirement. I am an old bachelor. I detest the world. I sit at home, quietly, in the evenings, and read, read, until my poor eyes give out. I have my dog, my cigarette, my 'Figaro!' I cannot live without my 'Figaro.' It is worth all our Russian gazettes put together. They are only made to put us off the track, as the people say here." She winked and laughed softly, as if at some amusing reminiscence. "And so you too are from America? His Excellency's niece,—cousin, did you say? Then you must have known a great American, one I have long desired to meet. You are probably intimately acquainted with Dom Pedro?"

"No," said the lady in violet, "I have not that honor."

"Ah, to be sure! How dull and stupid you must think me. You are from the north of America, from New York, I believe. I now recollect that you are not *au mieux* with the Brazilians; that you had that terrible and bloody war, and beat them badly too. I had forgotten. But, then," she added, politely, "it is so long ago you are too young to remember these things. I thought by this time all would be bridged over, but Southerners are always revengeful. And nature herself divides you from your Southern States. Look at your Isthmus of Panama!"

"You, monsieur," said the lady addressed, with quiet gravity, turning for the first time of her own accord and addressing me, "have probably had even greater facilities than madame to study our conflicts, since I believe you are a soldier as well as a diplomat. Do you not wonder at the continued animosity of the Brazilians?"

The Countess looked unconsciously from one to the other, awaiting my answer. Our eyes had met and mingled for a moment in the freemasonry of a mutual amusement. My own may have been too bold, for she blushed.

"I gave lectures to my young officers on your war, madame. Both sides fought well."

"You are encouraging," she replied, a little sarcastically I thought, and turned to have a foreign dignitary presented to her.

I was struck with her perfect composure, and also with her absolute indifference to myself. It piqued me into a desire to continue the conversation.

"Why did you come to Russia, madame?" I ventured to say to her later, handing her a cup of tea at her own request.

"To amuse myself."

"And are you amused?"

"No."

"Perhaps you are exacting?"

"Perhaps! I think myself very easily pleased."

"And you leave America like that? No duties . . . Nothing to detain you?"

"I never do my duty."

"Oh, madame!'

"And you?"

"I try to do mine."

"Why will you not undertake a new *devoir*, then?" and she looked at me aslant her little *voilette*, with a queer searching expression which held my own.

"And that is?"

"To help amuse me. I think you are not stupid. Nearly every one is stupid."

"How can you tell I am not stupid? You have not deigned to look at me once. I am lamentably dull."

"Really?"

"Yes; for although I have not taken my eyes from off your face since you entered, I do not know your name, or even whether I am addressing a married lady or a demoiselle."

"Ah! It makes no difference."

"Yes it does."

"Which do you think?"

"I think you are probably married."

"Why?"

"Because you have such diabolical *aplomb.*"

"And you think marriage leads to diabolical *dénouements?*"

"I know nothing about marriage, except what I hear from others, madame. I confess it is not encouraging."

"You are not married?"

"Do I look like a married person?"

"I have not examined you."

"Oh, yes, you have. You said I did not look stupid."

"One must say something."

"Thank you."

Mrs. North now moved again from the door, and her niece rose.

"I am really fatigued, *ma tante.* I shall ask you to excuse me and let me go and rest," and with a slight inclination of her head in my direction she swept from the room, dragging her violet skirts with a swish over the parquet floor.

"My niece has but lately arrived in Petersburg," said my hostess, apologetically. "She is mad, poor child, about art, and all these new sights. She has been at the galleries all day, and she is still tired from her long journey."

I bowed. "We diplomats, madame, are proverbially curious. Above all, we must know and remember names. May I ask you to tell me very distinctly the lady's name?"

"Mrs. Acton, Mrs. Lucien Acton."

"And is Monsieur Acton with you too?" I asked, "and shall I make his acquaintance?"

"My niece is a widow." Mrs. North sighed, —the perfunctory sigh with which the virtuous matron feels called upon to announce another's misfortune.

"Madame, I salute you," I said, shrinking somehow incomprehensibly from any further revelations, and taking my leave. Mr. North tried to detain me when I reached the hall. He is an agreeable man, but I made my escape, and, jumping into my sleigh, went on to the Kossecki's. I found quite a crowd there. It was *embêtant* in the extreme.

Certainly Mr. and Mrs. North seem excellent people. I must cultivate them.

January 22.—The expressions of the features, people say, of the eyes and mouth, denote a person's soul, yet one easily learns to conceal natural emotions under the facial mask. There are signs more unguarded, and hence more certain. A movement of the hips in walking, the position of an arm and of a hand are a revelation. Temperament is made clear to me often in a *dêmarche.* Charm, the *gewisses etwas*, has always seemed to me a spring from a heart full of passion, whether overflowing or concentrated and stifled. In either case, but particularly in the latter, it cannot be concealed; it breathes from the body, from the very garments.

Dark eyes are tell-tale. There is a long, half-shut, light eye which never reveals its secrets. The movements of graceful limbs betray far more. I think Mrs. Lucien Acton has such eyes. What an odd young woman!

It is a *praznik* here to-day. It is a *praznik* here every other day. Pavil has gone out and dragged most of the moujiks at his heels; that scamp, August, too, has managed to escape, and Gustav, forced to double duty, is trembling with suppressed fury.

I am obliged to attend the baptism of his Imperial Highness the little Grand Duke in the chapel of the Winter Palace. There is a great crowd in the streets. The baby drives in a coach drawn by six pure white horses, and behind comes the Grand Chamberlain. All about the royal carriage are mounted Cossacks. It is a pretty sight. Every one is in gala attire, and the court ladies wear the *kakochnik.*

The child is brought forward on a satin pillow embroidered in gold, by the Princess Nikitenko, with his godfathers following. The Imperial boy-choir sings in sweet unison, while the Pop immerses the child. The Czar then walks three times about the altar with his baby in his arms, and the whole affair breaks up with a general kissing; during which I felt very much left out in the cold, for nobody offered to kiss me.

Then the great breakfast at the palace, with its elaborate *menu,* where everybody's health was drunk, and every one seemed in good humor.

The pretty, heedless baby is already honorary colonel of half a dozen regiments. Good luck to him, poor little mortal! He needs kind thoughts and prayers, for what vicissitudes may he not encounter!

January 23.—Five hundred men and women, the latter splendid in their diamonds, the former in their uniforms and decorations, the cream of Petersburg society, gathered at the Winter Palace under the radiance of a hundred chandeliers. Within its gilded railing the orchestra regales us with sweet strains. In the rotunda and along the *galerie militaire*, a buffet where are served champagne frappé, fruits, ices, bonbons, and tea from smoking samovars, all served in Georgian silver, or upon massive gold plate.

Card-tables are disposed in the Arab Room. At ten the royalties arrive. The Emperor wears his uniform of the Cossack Guards, and the hereditary Grand Duke that of the Imperial Guard of Hussars. The Empress and her ladies of the Imperial family and household vie with each other in the magnificence of their toilets. They look like a flock of tropical birds.

Supper is served at one in the great banqueting-halls of the Nicholas and Jordanoffskaia, changed as by magic into delicious gardens of rare palms and exotic flowers. The Emperor, attended by Prince D., steps out among the tables to see that his guests are well served, while the Empress presides at her table surrounded by the Grand Duchesses, the ambassadors, and her ladies of honor.

A brilliant ball indeed, with many beautiful women, many distinguished men, light, jewels, music, laughter, magical effects, and supreme elegance. The Empress, ever affable and courteous, with her own beauty at its very best. So much for the frame. Now for the picture, and my own personal experiences. While I stood with a party of aides and courtiers awaiting the entrance of their Majesties, my eyes became fastened upon a pair of shoulders which rose out of their soft laces just in front of me, amid the crowd of ladies, wives and daughters of dignitaries, who were standing in readiness to make their courtesies to the approaching royalties.

I had never seen these shoulders, yet I felt a certain proprietorship in them. They seemed not strange to me, and their contemplation gave me the intimate delight which we feel in finding again, for an instant, some lost dream of youth or of romance. They were unencumbered by ornament of any sort, and this in a land of jewels where the women's heads and throats are fairly bowed under their weight of gems seemed to give an added charm and strength to their outline. I can fancy nothing more poetic than their slope, nothing more pure than the line of the neck from the tiny pink ear to the arm. It filled my sculptor's heart with delight. It is many years since I threw away my scalpel, that dear pastime of my boyish holidays, but the love of form is strong in me, and I found it here in its finest development.

The head, too, was haughtily held, with its

mignonne nuque and hair tossed up in a ray of light to the crown. The front locks are darker. I drew closer to drink in the perfume of beauty which seemed to radiate from the polished pink skin, for the complexion was not of ivory, but marbled, as if betokening a rich and generous vitality.

Did my breath ruffle her sensitiveness as I stood, closely buttoned into my full-dress uniform, my twenty-seven decorations ostentatiously placarded upon my manly breast, and the plume of my casque sweeping the floor close to her feet? At any rate, Mrs. Acton turned.

"Ah!" she said, "I *thought* it was you."

"I have been here close behind you for twenty minutes or more."

"And, pray, how were you occupied?"

"Contemplating your back, and conclusively persuaded that you had rested to some purpose."

"Why?"

"Why? Because you are so unspeakably fresh and radiant to-night."

"Does my back reveal all this? How very nice! I am amused, and that is the reason. Happiness is unbecoming! It makes one gaunt and hollow-eyed, like all the emotions; but amusement, pleasure, that is a woman's best atmosphere. It agrees with my health and my skin."

A disagreeable thought crossed my mind: I wondered what experiences Mrs. Acton had vaguely alluded to.

"I have never known happiness," I replied, not quite truthfully (and yet not all untruthfully either, for how pale it grows!), "and I am sick of . . . pleasure."

"I don't believe a word of what you say. You have tasted happiness, and you are not sick of pleasure. You *adore* pleasure;" she emphasized "adore" with a pretty *moue*. This made me laugh.

"You have to-night," she said, "the smile of a young tiger."

"If it is young, madame, man-like I pass over the less complimentary comparison."

"Why uncomplimentary? It pleases me.

Your smile is usually kindly and indulgent. To-night it is military and fierce. You are on parade. I admire it, your epaulets, and the feather in your hat."

"Take care, madame, you will have me assume a perpetual grin, and if I read you aright you will be the first to find it odious, for I feel sure that stereotyped men and things weary you, and that you quickly drive them away; then, besides, you are amusing yourself now immensely at my expense."

"Oh, no, when men grow tiresome I do not drive them away! I simply get up and leave them to themselves."

"I was very tiresome, then, the other day at the legation?"

"Very."

I felt as piqued as an awkward school-boy. She noticed my gloomy visage, and made instant amends for her raillery by looking up at me with a lovely smile.

"Here," she said, "is just the type you admire, I am certain. This tall woman entering on this officer's arm: large black eyes, ar eagle's nose, a high forehead, and a—moustache!"

"Effectively Madame Lowenstein is very handsome. That gentleman is her husband."

"They seem to have a great deal to say to each other. She looks annoyed and yet deprecating."

"Of course; she speaks to him with that mixture of irritability and compunction to which women treat the men they habitually deceive. Here is her lover. Now watch their little manœuvres."

"Ah, monsieur, you make me afraid of you!"

"I wish that I could. So you do not admire feminine moustaches?"

"Do you?"

"Immensely. A little down on a red upper lip is not without allurement."

"In America it would be called a defect."

"Ah, you are a young people! We need spicier things to suit our vitiated and perverted taste."

"I dislike to be laughed at."

"I was never more serious in my life."

Then the Imperial party entered and Lady Xavier carried away Mrs. Acton to be presented to their Majesties.

I stood against a pillar and watched the pageant. There was a good deal of vexation, I fear, in my manner, when Prince D. tapped me on the shoulder and issued his commands that I should engage the Princess Nikitenko for the Mazurka, that wild coquettish dance, little suited to the mature proportions of my partner. But I was caught.

For nearly an hour I lost sight of Madame Acton while I piloted my stout partner through the intricate figures. I heard distant rumors, however, of her successes. Several women asked me if I had seen the *Américaine*, and some men in passing urged me to present them.

When the Mazurka was over, with indecent haste I bowed to my Princess and wandered forth in search of her. I found her at last in the conservatory amid a forest of plants and shrubs, half hidden. Berg was leaning over her, and a certain Circassian prince of my acquaintance, brave in his purple velvet doublet tipped with sables, his sabre and jewelled poniard, was holding her cup of yellow *chay.* Did she look a little bored, or was it only my fatuity which fancied that her fair face lighted up in welcome at my approach?

"Well, *mon cher,*" I said to Prince Savfet, "another beautiful woman has succumbed to your poniard and those furs of yours. And he has the folly to believe, madame, that it is all for his *beaux yeux.*"

"Why, this lady has ill-treated me, called me a savage, and refused to take my arm to supper," answered Savfet, looking down at Mrs. Acton with the dreamy far-away eyes of his race.

Berg certainly has a most indecent tone with women. I could have fairly struck him in the face for the way he was devouring Mrs. Acton with his eyes. The devil take his impudence! And she, to be sure, careless and languid, indifferent,—who knows, perhaps pleased! I notice the greater the lady and the more refined, the less mindful she is of such bold glances. Can it be possible they do not detect the lurking insult in such homage!

Every woman seems to prefer a compliment to her beauty than to her intellect, to her fascination than to her moral qualities. I am positive that the Empress is just the same. They absolutely like it, and there is some truth in poor Nathalie's cynicism.

After a few more words of badinage I offered her my arm. "Come," I said, authoritatively, and she came. Away from the others, her graceful swaying figure balanced on my arm by the light touch of a long gloved hand, the little curls of her dark hair just brushing against the gold of my epaulet, we passed down the stately halls together, reflected in a hundred mirrors. People asked who was this tall stranger in her exquisite pale draperies which fell about her like the *peplum* of a Greek goddess.

She was very quiet; not in the least dazzled by anything that she saw; much more of a princess than the real ones, I thought, with her elegant *insouciance;* an American princess of a subtler quality. I remembered poor Flavie with her unkempt locks and her petty economies!

Of course this can be nothing serious, only . . . I wonder who and what she is. I hardly know what we talked about. I only know that her heart beat close to mine, and made its pulses warmer. I spoke to her of the approaching masked ball.

"My uncle would not approve," she said.

"Then do not tell him; only go!"

"What vile advice! Of course to go clandestinely would be a great inducement. But I should have fancied you too conservative to give a young woman such evil counsel, particularly when her nature inclines her to follow it. What! deceive my good kind uncle who is so indulgent to me?"

"So you think me conservative?"

"I know that you are."

"Think what you will, only promise me you will go to the masked ball," I said, hotly.

"There are things, monsieur, one does, and one does not say."

She is enchanting!

That was a good ball!

January 24.—At the Anichkoff this morning I found the Czar playing at snowballs with his boys in the palace court-yard. The Empress smiled down at them from her windows: a pretty family group.

There is to be a review on the 26th, in my honor, I believe. To-day no one seems in the mood to discuss state problems. Every one is lazy, still more or less in a *praznik* humor. The review, if this moderate weather continues, will take place on the Siemnié Dovarietz Square. The snow is falling; this queer Russian snow, like salt, sifting, drifting down. No storm, no wind; all swift and silent. It never melts here, and they care for the streets, so that the walking is clean and hard.

I am better off than I expected. I like my rooms. I think I can help my government. I am rid of the Flavie-Harnay complications. My sovereign seems contented with my reports.

My mornings are spent at my work and in attendance at the palace or at the foreign ministry. At three the twilight creeps on; one winds one's lamp and then goes out visiting until dinner-time. Then a ball or a play and supper. They are beginning to organize *troïka* parties. Mrs. Acton should try the *troïka.* She would like the rush of it, if she be a true American. Only to think that I do not even know her *petit nom!* I will wager it is a peculiar one, like herself. I will not forget to ask her.

The streets are bright to-day with walkers and equipages. I enjoy the excitement of this rapid driving through the nipping air. It is capital fun. One forgets one is living on a morass. How despotic was the construction of Petersburg! One man's isolated act, building on a hopeless waste, surrounded by endless uncultivated plains. Who can tell how much of the mystic sadness, the strength and patience of the Russian of to-day may be traced to the fact that his culture and his government come to him from this Baltic-girt ice-bound city, spring from a cruel fight with the forces of nature, and are in their very birth a sacrifice? Petersburg was a work of genius. To create is to suffer!

Later.—It is decided that all the military shall go to the masked ball *en bourgeois.* Women have told me I looked well in citizen's clothes. If Mrs. Acton be there will she recognize me, I wonder! These were my reflections as I struggled into my dress suit and white cravat. To myself I looked like a dissipated old dandy. *Ohimè!*

What a queer effect a *bal masqué* produces upon one's first entrance! The *Tziganes* had been hired to amuse the company, and were still singing their wild ditties when I arrived about one o'clock. There seemed to be much gayety among the merry maskers, but somehow I could not feel the slightest breath of excitement or of *entrain.* I leaned wearily for some time against a column, watching the varied scene, when suddenly Berg passed and jostled me in the crowd, with a tall domino upon his arm, to whom he was discoursing in animated Russian. It impressed me that she did not understand a word that he was saying. She seemed listless and *distraite.*

She wore a long rich gray garment, made like a coat, with high puffed sleeves, opening over a pale yellow skirt; it was richly embroidered about the throat and wrists. Her small head was closely shrouded in white laces, and she wore a yellow satin mask. It was a striking costume enough, and people turned to look at her. It was made so as to disguise somewhat, although it could not conceal the lines of her figure.

After passing me she seemed to hesitate a moment, then left Berg abruptly, and, turning away from him and gliding swiftly up to me, slipped her hand through my arm. The Grand Dukes stopped to speak with me at this moment, and addressed a few words of gallantry to my companion, but she did not deign to reply to them, only clinging a little closer to my side.

"Whom do you seek?" she whispered at last, in an unnatural key.

"Really," I said, nonchalantly, "I am expecting no one. Petersburg holds few interests to me, and I merely looked in at this ball as a civility to our hostess, Madame Soltikoff."

She pulled a pencil out from the gold girdle which was drawn about her waist, and a tiny ivory tablet, and wrote, "I was admiring your enthusiasm!"

"My enthusiasm?"

"Yes. You were looking about with an expression of idiotic pleasure when I rescued you from your contemplations."

"Seriously, have you seen any woman here to-night whose masked loveliness seemed to attract me? Did I look as if I were waiting for some one?"

She shrugged her shoulders, and did not reply.

While we had so spoken we had wandered from among the throng which gathered about the dance-rooms and the buffets, into a little boudoir whose cool loveliness had not yet been invaded. My companion drew her arm from mine, and seated herself with a sigh upon a low couch which stood invitingly near. It was wide enough for two, although not very wide, and I slipped into it by her side. All the *ennui* was gone now.

"How nice you look like that, dressed like a man of the world," she said.

"What! really?" I felt myself blushing with delight,—turning mahogany color, as my brother Marc fraternally remarks, when I am flushed with sentiment.

"And you?" I said, secretly exhilarated by the contact of her shoulder, and a queer delicious perfume which came to me in wafts from her laces and hair, and which made me just a bit dizzy,—"and you, are you very beautiful to-night?"

For all answer she drew off her gloves from her strong, white hands, and, disentangling her mask, pulled it off suddenly and cast it from her upon a distant seat.

"Ugh!" she said, raising her arms to re-adjust her disordered headgear, and, with a funny little groan, "I was half stifled;" and she drew the lace back tightly across her forehead just above her brow. Her profile seen thus coiffed like an Eastern woman struck me with its delicacy and fineness. Her cheeks were all aflame from the heat of the mask, her half-open lips looked red like blood. How little women know the power of such disarray! She was an entirely different being from the lady of the court ball; she seemed much nearer to me. A wild desire to crush and hurt her seized me, to deepen the flame on her cheeks, to awaken some sentiment of love or of hate in those sleepy eyes.

"You are a pretty woman," I said, scanning her critically from head to foot with an impertinent audacity at which I myself marvelled, "but you are scarcely beautiful. Not one of those women of whom one says, 'She is possessed of a dazzling seduction.'"

She remained silent for a moment and then languidly turned towards me, raising her face up almost to the level of my own. She opened those half-closed lids at last widely upon me and shot into my soul a glance whose lightning ran through my senses like fire. I can give no idea to any one who has never seen this expression of Mrs. Acton's face, of its peculiar power. There would indeed be a lack of *pudeur* if a woman could so unveil herself often, and she inspires me with enough confidence to believe that to the many it has never been revealed. All the anguish, all the hallucinations of a man's maddest desire leaped within me into life. In another moment the lids were lowered, with their impenetrable veil, and a sense of loss fell upon me.

"Are you sure?" she asked, and her voice was but a breath.

"No."

She had resented my insolence with her own weapons. She was avenged. At this moment peals of boisterous laughter broke upon our solitude. Lady Xavier, ill concealed under her red domino, followed by half a dozen young attachés, the Princesse Nikitenko, my late partner of the dance, and old Prince Suwaroff swarmed into our boudoir. Distant music followed faintly after them.

It is needless to say that for the rest of the evening I remained spellbound by her side. Before we parted I asked her her name. "Daphne," she said.

When I reached my rooms I tried to reason with and laugh at myself. Nothing could be more unfortunate and inopportune for me than a serious preference. Mrs. Acton is either a very ingenuous, innocent, and imprudent young woman, or a diabolic coquette whom one had better avoid. I shall not try to solve the enigma. Of course I am not a beardless boy or a stick, to remain insensible under such a challenge. I am forced, unwillingly, to admit that she is eminently occupying and disturbing; that she is not insignificant, like the majority of her sex, nor one of those women with whom one can "amuse" one's self, and that she is distinctly a danger; yet I propose to remain heart-free, and I fancy that the wiser course will be to give a wide berth to this extraordinary enchantress.

January 26.—"The street fires are lit, Herr Graff," said Gustav, when he opened my curtains, "and we have four degrees."

This looks hopeful for the review to-morrow. Frozen noses and feet in the service of Mars! but when I got a little sunshine into my room, and a cup of coffee and my *kalatch*, it was not so very terrible. A strong smell of *chypre* pervaded my breakfast-tray, and under my official mail and despatches lay a tiny pink note, with a silver heart pierced by a dagger on the envelope. It was a rodomontade from Madame Nathalie,—the third that I have received since her visit. I wonder how much longer this bombardment will continue! She considers I have treated her ill; I have not called upon her; I have not been to the theatre; I have not answered her letters; I have not lent her the books she asked for,—*Mein Gott!* what books? Finally, she admires and reveres me. When will I let her come to breakfast again? Then I find a tiny, timid letter from Flavie. She has had the brilliants taken from the book-mark I sent her and set into a ring. The devil take her and her mawkish folly! I am her true, best, only friend,—except Madame Harnay, the old hypocrite! Papa has the gout, and is, oh, so cross! And will I write soon? She remains devotedly my friend, Flavie, Princesse of S. V.

So much for the ladies. Of the contents of my official mail I write nothing here. Stoffel has not understood my last letters. *Bon!* it is all to do over. I feel dull and have a cold in my head. I don don my shuba and goloshes and go out for a walk, but I am lazy and tired, and I hail an *isvoztchik* at the street corner. The *isvoztchik* is so fat that he keeps my feet warm, and as we dash at full speed through the *Fourschtatskaia* I have an experience: all the blood leaves my heart suddenly,—it gives a wild leap. My lips become dry and parched; fingers of iron seem to be clutching at my throat; my limbs grow numb and tremble. As suddenly these peculiarly unpleasant sensations subside, and leave me a helpless limp mass clinging to the strap of my *çani* with one hand and to my driver's belt with the other. He cries "*Birigui!*" to a hapless passer-by, shows his teeth, and urges on his horse, thinking undoubtedly that the *Barin* is in a hurry.

Now what was the cause of this curious nervous spasm? Simply this: I caught sight of a brown shuba, bordered with dark furs, and enveloping the slender form of . . .

Is it possible? No, it is not possible, yet no man of my years is entirely a novice to such symptoms. She was walking with her aunt. They were entirely unconscious of my presence. But is it, or is it not, as I say, possible that such a slight cause should produce such a powerful effect, and so upset a person of my health and vigor? What can it mean?

If I were younger, if I was not disillusioned, if I had not thoroughly acknowledged my satiety of life, I should say . . . but, no! At any rate, it is an extremely peculiar psychological fact. I ordered my *isvoztchik* to drive on anywhere, everywhere. We seemed to go very far; my teeth chattered. Finally he pulls up at a monastery porch, and mumbles in Russian that there is a fine "something" going on in there which the *Barin* should see for himself. I spring out of the sleigh into a snow-drift, uncover, and go in. The Sisters are holding a service, and the church is dark, save where the wax-lights glitter at the altar and before the sacred Icons. This is, I perceive, a very aristocratic sisterhood, of whom I think I have heard it said that a demoiselle Oblensky is Mother Superior. Many of them show their birth and elegance even under the austere garb in which they move and stand in the nave together. The music is low and plaintive. I am offered a lighted taper; I take it; at a certain moment we all turn them down, and they go out. I kneel for a moment before I go forth into the sunshine. I utter no prayer, but calm has returned to me; the fever is past. Thank God!

What could they be doing in the *Fourschtatskaia* at that hour? Perhaps they were going to breakfast with the Princesse Vera, who lives at No. 30. It is the most ridiculous nonsense! I never heard of such a thing! I mean . . . I don't know what I mean!

When I come in, instead of settling down to business and to the gruesomeness of my reports, I am utterly restless and demoralized, and I finally write a short note and direct it to Madame Lucien Acton, Americanskoe Posolstvo. No woman has ever before so interfered with my duties. I do not say this boastfully, for I have not had a high enough opinion of the sex.

My note is merely a formal announcement that I shall do myself the honor of calling upon her at five, and a request that she will let me know if she can receive me. As there is no earthly visible reason why I should not call at the legation, it will be very evident to her that my letter is only a trap to secure something from her,—anything. A silly, vulgar trap, written over three times, endlessly corrected, and awkwardly enough expressed in the end. My charming enemy, however, does not fall into the trap. I begin to think her unattractively clever. I wait and

I wait. Narishkine is announced, and, as he talks, I watch the door. Gustav enters with some eau de Seltz.

"Quick!" I say, "the answer to that note!"

Gustav stares, Narishkine stares, I stare.

"There is no note; they said there was no answer."

Four o'clock comes. N. takes his departure. I make an excuse to accompany him as far as the porter's lodge. I tap at the latter's window.

"Has a note come for me? *Adno pismo? adno pismo?*"

"*Nieto pismo!*"

I seize him roughly by the shoulder and shake him.

"Quick," I say, "fellow, disgorge that note you must be hiding somewhere!"

He disengages himself, rubs his head, and evidently believes the *Barin* is crazy or drunk. I mumble a feeble apology, say there is a mistake, and give him three rubles. He takes the money and closes the door carefully, putting himself well out of my reach, and peep-

f

ing cautiously out through the pane of glass at which he reconnoitres the campaign of life, observes me furtively as I go back slowly to my apartments.

I have an extremely bad quarter of an hour. Has she taken offence? Was she really angry last night? and did she only conceal her vexation for future revenge? Was my note an improper one? How can I tell what her point of view upon these questions may be? Too warm? Too cold? Five o'clock comes, and I have lashed myself into a condition of miserable anxiety. I order my sleigh and am driven to the legation.

"Is Madame Acton at home?" I am too impatient even to name Mrs. North.

"*Oui, monsieur.*" The Chasseur Alexei smiles and ushers me up-stairs. "Madame is in the boudoir." He pushes the heavy portière slightly, and, announcing me, retires.

I enter, but there is no goddess in the temple; only a scent of lilies, and a bright fire in the open hearth. I am about to turn and call him back, when through another curtain which hangs before a smaller side door I hear a few chords struck on a piano and a rich voice breaks forth into song.

I have found the song since, and I give it here as it fell for the first time upon my ears:

"Bois frissonnant, ciel étoilé,
Mon bien aimé s'en est allé,
Emportant mon cœur désolé.

"Le premier jour qu'il vint ici
Mon âme fut à sa merci;
De fierté je n'eus plus souci.

"Mon regard était plein d'aveux,
Il me prit dans ses bras nerveux,
Et me baisa près des cheveux.

"J'en eus un long frémissement,
Et puis, je ne sais plus comment
Il est devenu mon amant.

"Je lui disais, 'Tu m'aimeras
Aussi longtemps que tu pourras?'
Je ne dormais bien qu'en ses bras.

"Mais lui, sentant son cœur éteint,
S'en est allé, l'autre matin,
Sans moi! dans un pays lointain."

Oh, who could paint the inexpressive recklessness with which this daughter of the Puritans sang! The timid awakening of the first verse, the pent-up fires of the second, the agony and despair of the last.

I stood rooted to the spot, and my heart fluttered with pleasure, like a school-boy's, but the blood which flowed through my veins was not a boy's. As I listened to the intoxicating accents of this creature, who was so near me and yet unconscious of my presence, I pictured to myself that in a moment she would stand beside me, when I too, like the lover in the song, would seize her in my arms and kiss her hair. I wanted to wring and hurt her long fingers in mine, to crush her close against me, until she shrunk and cried for mercy.

Mine is not a fierce nature. On the field my heart bleeds for the wounded enemy. I am kind and tender with women, but I can hardly depict the sentiment Daphne had awakened in me by her strange singing. The curtain was suddenly pulled back with an energetic hand.

"*Tiens!*" she said, entering; "is it you?"

I thought I had never seen her looking so unapproachable, and my heart sank. Even her dress was discouraging. She was clad all in black, in sombre folds of heavy plush, which threw out in startling contrast the fairness of her throat. She motioned me to a seat, and herself assumed a somewhat studied majesty of pose in a corner of the sofa, which was drawn close to the fire. Her eyes were cold, and rested upon me like ice.

"Why did you not answer my letter?" I began, with a certain bitterness, asking myself if this woman and the songstress could indeed be the same.

"Your letter? . . . Oh!—did it require a reply?"

I thought of my restless afternoon, and groaned.

"Are you ill?" she said.

"Yes," I said, "very."

She laughed. "Why, you look so white you really quite frighten me."

"Do I, madame? I did not imagine myself

very alarming. I assure you you are quite safe."

She leaned her head back against the laces of a soft cushion, with her chin up a little and the firelight on her bright brown hair.

"What news from . . . your court?" she asked, lightly, with that gift of changing the subject which is so peculiarly her own, and as if desiring to avoid personal talk.

"Oh, nothing in particular," I replied, having regained my *sang-froid;* "only I am always anxious about my adored Emperor. If he should be taken——"

"He is very old," she said, laconically.

"Of course," I answered, a little angered at her manner, "it is impossible for an American to enter into our feelings."

"Yes, thank God," she said, dryly, and in a staccato voice which I did not recognize as her own. "We are not an *exalté* people."

"That means, I suppose, that we *are?*"

She made no reply.

"My Emperor has been for many years the

one great pure affection of my heart, and of his people's," I added, a little pompously.

"A peculiar affection, to wish him to suffer."

"*I* wish him to suffer?"

"Why, yes," she said, impatiently. "Do you suppose life is amusing when one is nearly one hundred, and one has no teeth nor hair nor anything? Only family quarrels and political brawls for one's entertainment?"

"You are hard upon us, madame."

She smothered a yawn behind her hand.

"For myself I like the display and splendors of a court," she continued; "but the people all seem puppets and mountebanks made for my especial entertainment, and they impress me, a republican, with not one whit of reverence or awe. I suppose that is hard for them and their sycophants. Why, since I left America I have only met one *man!*"

"I fear I am . . . boring you," I said, stiffly. "Pardon me if I intruded;" and I rose. Her tone was so disobliging that I could hardly remain with dignity.

"I suppose if you, for instance," she continued, not noticing my movement, "were ordered to kill some one, or to . . . marry some one, you would have to obey instantly."

I could not help laughing. "If I had the right to tell you of a recent episode of my career, you would absolve me at least from the charge of such abject servitude."

"I don't doubt it would be very interesting," she answered, mockingly.

"But," I continued, irritated, "while I am not too proud to be one of the puppets to dance for your amusement, I fear at present I am a failure even in this rôle, and will therefore bid you good-evening."

"You will not wait for tea?" she said, with a slight compunction. As I weakly hesitated a moment she made a gesture as if she would detain me.

"Let us speak seriously for a moment, madame," I said. "Men of my world have told me I possessed tact. The mission which brought me to this country is one which requires discreet and delicate handling. It could hardly have been intrusted to a blunderer, but in you I find a riddle that baffles all my experience, and while it is undoubtedly well worth the reading, I fear I have not the requisite courage to attempt the task. All the odds would be against me. I will leave its unravelling to the one fortunate '*man*' to whom you alluded a moment since."

"He does not care," she faltered, faintly.

"That," I replied, "is hardly possible, if your eyes have rested upon him, in approval, even for a passing moment. Of myself I have nothing further to say. When you did not deign to answer my note, the cruelty and neglect should have opened my eyes to the fact that I am importunate and unwelcome. Ah, if you only knew, madame, with what respect and humility it was written, and with what impatience and longing I awaited your bidding!"

"I take no lessons in behavior!" She looked at me haughtily, but I noticed that her lips trembled.

"I offer none," I replied. "I only withdraw. I came, unbidden, because to stay away seemed death, and, just now, when I listened to your beautiful voice, I thought myself in heaven. My mind was full of thoughts I wished to express to you. My heart, oh, I wish that my heart might have been bared to you! It was overflowing! I had so much to say to you, but the disillusion and disappointment have been complete." An extraordinary emotion shook me. I turned away from her that she should not see how unmanned I was.

When I looked at her again, imagine my amazement when suddenly, yes, there could be no doubt, two large drops detached themselves from under her eyelashes, ran slowly down her cheeks and fell upon her hands, which were clasped together across her knees.

I sprang towards her, my sword clanking against her chair. "My child," I said, "have I wounded you?"

"Count Berg," announced Alexei; and then others came: Mrs. North, complaining of the cold; Mr. North, talkative and a trifle prolix; Madame de Barythine, still gossiping about her niece Wasia, the Oblensky diamonds, and her dead lord's mausoleum.

I sat rooted to the spot, meekly absorbing tea and little cakes, agreeing with everybody, feebly, mildly, unutterably imbecile. Mrs. Acton, on the contrary, was sparkling, original, and gay, developing those peculiar gifts and graces which fit her so eminently for the salon. She possesses to a rare degree the facility of turning from the discussion of serious topics to that of adorable fatuities.

I remember some remarks she made apropos of the Latin and Anglo-Saxon races: "I like the Russians," she was saying, "because they are nearer to me. The Slav I can understand, but between us and the Latins is a great gulf, impassable. Why, look at it! The marriages are hardly ever happy, and even friendships are at best halt and lame. We shall always speak a different language, and forever misunderstand each other. Between myself, *ma tante*," she said, turning to Mrs. North, "and my friend, Heloise de St. Pierre, for instance, there is a sincere affection, much mutual regard, and yet with it all a secret antagonism which I have always felt will explode some day and bury all our past beneath its ruins. They are prudent, narrow, calculating. We are reckless, wild, fond of change. It is not only the education and the customs, but the temperament is absolutely different."

Berg, with his mouth full of cake, thought all humanity was the same; only individual sentiments differed. He was glad, however, that he was himself a Saxon, and therefore satisfactory, and fully able to appreciate Mrs. Acton's brilliant opinions; to which she replied, "Ah!" with a sarcastic inflection which did me good.

I left by and by with the others, merely exchanging a formal farewell with Mrs. Acton. When I got into the street I put my hand to my head. One thing is certain: I shall be much happier. The struggle is over: I love her!

I remembered that I had always thought what I desired and admired most in a woman was great simplicity, and—I laughed.

January 26.—Strangers meet, they gauge each other: one is master.

More courage is required to avoid temptation than to give it battle. Love is *not* a malady, but a plenitude of health, of happy body and mind. Why, then, try to escape? Is it not better to love even unwisely than . . . not? How glorious to hope and to fear! Some women have an eloquence in their whole persons which touches and sets vibrating chords lying wrapped away in the veriest secret recesses of the heart, but women are *bourgeoises* in their judgments of each other. They cannot understand. They think beauty or wit will master us. No, mesdames, the mystery lies deeper. What masters us is the promise that some women seem to make to us,—the promise to slake that thirst for rapture which every imaginative soul craves. Yet—do we really possess them as wholly as those who promise less? and will they not keep from us an eternal secret,—a something altogether vague and illusive? What is even the closest nearness of two bodies if the essence escapes?

Do we know for five minutes at a time what these creatures are thinking about?

What pain for a passionate heart to know itself insufficient for the heart it loves! Mediocre people have no such fears. They come to the great feasts of life without humility and without distrust; but people of high, delicate organizations and sensitive pride turn with question from the banquet.

One thing I have learned: passion is patient. Those who say otherwise lie!

I walked last night in a distant *dvor*, far from the fashionable thoroughfares. I like to see near at hand, to study, this strange, *triste*, laborious people, to mix in the motley crowd of these men, innocent of bath and sponge, their blood burned with *vodka*, reeking with perspiration, with the rank odors of old sheepskin garments, and with their wild matted hair and beards, from which shine out their sad searching eyes. The girls and women, with their large hips and bosoms, are straight, powerful, strong-handed, with foolish mouths, and teeth whose early decay is doubtless due to the exposure of sleeping in damp courtyards and to drinking the marsh waters. I have always had this taste for contact with absolute nature. I am a romantic realist. I like to peer into their rugged faces. There is something mystic about the Russian to me; even among the most miserable and ignorant there is an element of spirituality, a certain width with a lack of clearness. They are as misty as their own horizons. Some clever man has said, "Place the Latin and the Slav before a spy-glass: the former shortens it to suit his vision, sees clearly and distinctly; the latter develops the full force of the lens, and reaches farther, but more confusedly." So when we study them we must employ their own methods.

To-day took place the review in my honor. The troops formed on the Winter Palace square, every one in full-dress uniform, bright arms, and the horses' shoes sparkling like polished glass on the silvery snow, which flew up like dust under a hundred hoofs,—a fine effect! There was a pink glow on St. Isaac's dome, the lovely spire of the Admiralty, the casques and cuirasses of the troops, the Dragoons, Chevalier Gardes, Garde à Cheval, the most aristocratic regiment of Russia, Cuirassiers, Lancers, the Infantry Preobrajensky, and the soldiers of Paul, with their flat noses and big copper hats,—a proud military array, indeed, upon which Western Europe may well keep its eyes. To quake is folly, but vigilance will be wise. A magnificent spectacle, this defile of the forces of a vast, picturesque empire.

I rode close to the Czar, his aides following. We salute the Empress and her ladies, who are at a window of the palace. "Good-day, my children!" cries the "Little Father" to his soldiers. The bands strike up as the Czar dashes past on his great white horse. After the inspection the movements begin. We draw up at the grand entrance, and when all is over we adjourn to *déjeuner*, at which, among other dishes, a splendid sturgeon is brought in by half a dozen servants on a gold dish. It was stuffed with a sort of gruel which the peasants eat, and which the courtiers do not disdain.

Earlier in the day, as I had driven away to get my horse at the barracks, I had met the chasseur of the American legation. He hailed my man Ivan, stopped my sleigh, and gave me a little note. In romances people anticipate such delights; in real life they are always unexpected. I imagined the missive to be a formal invitation from Mrs. North to join a *troïka* party the ladies were planning, but the golden crest and the bold, rather illegible handwriting were unknown to me. I unsealed it. There were only a few words:

"We are at a window of the État Major, and shall look for a salute from you when you ride past.

"When you meet my uncle at the breakfast after the review, speak with him about our *troïka* drive. He will tell you all the arrangements.

"Am I forgiven?

"DAPHNE ACTON."

I put Daphne's letter in my breast that it

might keep my heart warm, oh, so warm! I did not suffer from the cold. I saw my joy at the window, and sent her a salute. What my soul sent to her I will not write.

January 29.—I met Mr. North at the palace breakfast after the review, and while we smoked he drew me apart and told me that the ladies wished me to be at the legation at ten o'clock that evening; that the party would meet there and drive in four *troïkas* to supper at the Islands; rooms had been engaged, and even music in case we liked to dance. We might, if the people came punctually enough, have time to stop at the Ice Palace, which his niece had not seen, etc. He seems an excellent man.

I was at the legation as the clock struck the hour. I had heralded my arrival to Mrs. Acton by a gift of lilies.

"Military punctuality," cried Mrs. North, turning with cordial greeting from her occupation of heaping some roses upon one of the innumerable *étagères* which are placed about this charming room.

She was alone; how glad I was of it! If only fifteen minutes *tête-à-tête* were accorded to us I should at least know some things which I waited to hear with almost febrile anxiety. Is it possible that this lady had already guessed what occupied my thought! Had she read in my dark visage the secret of my growing infatuation? They say that the Yankees are a shrewd race. Certain it is that while she passed hither and thither among her flowers, with considerable tact, and good breeding, she managed to give me a sketch of her niece's past.

"Daphne," she began, "is late, as usual. Ten minutes ago she was writing letters in her *robe de chambre*, with her hair on her shoulders. She is the most extraordinary mixture of languor and of energy, calmness, and unrest. I am sure I don't know where she gets her peculiarities. I tell Mr. North his family is entirely prosaic, commonplace, and—as people should be,—Mrs. Acton, you know, is his niece, not mine."

I was so absorbed in her words that as she

turned to look at me a moment I saw her smile.

"You are a good listener," she said. "You see I take it for granted that she interests you, as she does every one else. Shall I tell you something of her strange life?"

I only bowed. I found it impossible to speak.

"Daphne was educated in Europe, principally in France, where her mother made her home for several years. They had every advantage, she and her sister. Daphne's mother had married a man of very large wealth; he was a power in our world of finance. All our men, you know, have a serious career. There came a 'panic,' as we call such a crisis in America, and he lost everything.

"I think the loss of prestige was more bitter to him than that of wealth, for he had prided himself on his great capacity; every one had looked up to him. His wife and daughters were in Europe at the time. They hurried home. Daphne was a very romantic girl;

she had not yet been into the world. She was such a child! I can only thus explain her marriage; it is the only excuse. Lucien Acton was the intimate friend of Daphne's father, a rich man, unmarried, and his principal creditor. That was the worst of it. In the crash others had suffered.

"Mr. Acton was ill then with some incurable malady; his physicians had declared he could not live many months. He had no near relatives, and he desired to leave all his fortune to his friend, to forgive the debt, and make generous loans immediately. My brother-in-law would not hear of this. He was a proud man, and independent. Mr. Acton had known them all very intimately for years. He had always been fond of the children, particularly of Daphne. He had been much with them abroad, and had interested himself in their education. I myself never liked him, but he was very clever. At last he said, 'Give me Daphne! She shall be my child for a few days, and then my widow. That will arrange everything. It was so like

Lucien Acton. He was a cynic. He always thought nothing mattered.

"Unfortunately, Daphne's mother, half-laughingly, said to the girl, 'What do you think? Mr. Acton suggests . . . that you should marry him. He then could help papa, and it would look less badly to the world. What a strange idea!' I say 'unfortunately,' for the words did not fall on unresponsive ears. In the girl's brain they took seed and flourished. I cannot go into particulars. She ran away to him, to his rooms, one night, with her old nurse, who wickedly abetted her, and another witness, and they sent for a clergyman and were married. I consider it a crime on Mr. Acton's part. I never could understand. I sometimes wonder if he were desperately in love with her and determined that she should have his name. I don't know anything about it. Daphne never opens her lips. People say he meant well,—that he felt sure he could not live six weeks. The most awful thing is that he got better and lived . . . not six weeks, but ten years! although always a cripple."

My heart was on fire; my hands like ice.

"And her parents?" I asked, coldly.

"They were violently angry at first, and for a long time, but . . . what will you have?"

Mrs. North put a finishing touch to a vase upon the mantel-piece at my side, and then drew away to see its effect.

"The most intense *rancunes*," she continued, leaving her flowers to seat herself near the fire at my side,—"the most intense *rancunes* have to end. We are all weak and vacillating at the best, and—shall I admit it?—not insensible, I fear, to material success. When Daphne developed into a leader of fashion, and was distinguished and sought after by all the most elegant men and women of her coterie, as the years went by, all had to be accepted. I am afraid that perhaps they felt just a little pride in her. She made her young sister the fashion, too, and married her well.

"I must say Lucien Acton behaved nobly to her. 'My dear,' he used to say, 'I can never forgive myself for not having died when

I ought, but you will bear with me to the end. It cannot be for long.' *On dit* that all their relationship consisted in his being wheeled into her boudoir to see her dressed for balls. He was very undemonstrative in his manner towards her. He would coldly criticise her gowns and her jewels; tell her if she was too *décolletée*, give her a little worldly advice as to behavior, and then be wheeled out again by his valet. But I think there was a much deeper influence, and a much more unfortunate one; his was a very brilliant mind, and influenced hers. I think he gave her false ideas of life. It was all very unnatural. She was too young to be fed upon the mental pabulum which suited a man of his years and intellect. He was a man of no religion. His principal recreation from his literary pursuits, to which he dedicated the greater part of his hours, was cards. He used to have his friends every afternoon, Sundays included, and they passed all the late afternoons at play. I am very old-fashioned; I think such things quite wicked and dreadful. Yet I am told that his crippled condition was owing to an injury to his spine sustained when he saved the lives of some children from a fire at a summer watering-place. So evidently the man had fine traits of character. One must not be too harsh." Mrs. North sighed.

"He was certainly an agreeable companion, a thorough man of the world, polished as steel. I must admit that he placed Daphne in a splendid position, and she never would hear one word. She revered his cleverness, and thought him the very embodiment of honor. Of course she had imagined an act of romantic heroism in sacrificing herself for her family. Young girls have these silly fancies. When it was not appreciated she felt bitterly towards them, and it took some time for the breach to heal. But, as I say, we all have a worldly side. I may do them injustice, but I think Daphne's success dazzled them at last, and had much to do with the final reconciliation which they earnestly sought. Her life certainly did not *look* a failure. He gave her absolute liberty."

I listened breathlessly, in momentary dread of interruption.

"There is not much more to tell. He died three years ago. She is very rich. I admire Daphne excessively. I think her most attractive. She entirely fascinates me. I am not sure that I love her. I should rather pity any man who did." Here Mrs. North stopped short with a little nervous laughter, and there was a pause. Did its pulsations hold a warning? After a moment she continued:

"I hope she will find happiness. She has had what the world calls luck, but we women know the difference. I hope she will marry."

"Who would dare?" I murmured.

"Ah!" she replied; "some very simple person with no theories about her, with no intricacies; that would be the best. Some good practical American, I hope. They, after all, understand their own women the best."

"Few men of any nation," I replied, somewhat nettled, I know not why, "could boast of fathoming such a nature."

"Yes, she is difficult to read. It would be

better for the man not to try; only to give her affection, a lot of affection, and not attempt to control her. You foreigners," she went on, smiling, "are neglectful when you don't love, and far too exacting when you do."

"I should be very exacting."

"I am sure of it," said Mrs. North.

"I think the man should be the head, should guide."

"Ah! We should call that old-fashioned. We American women are progressive and *entêtées*." And then a silence fell between us, a somewhat awkward one. It was interrupted by the entrance of Mrs. Acton.

As she tripped across the threshold the words, "He gave her entire liberty," were still ringing in my ears. "Liberty?" Yes; what had she done with it? I asked myself.

Notwithstanding her aunt's suggestion that from her character surprises might be anticipated, when I looked up at her I felt a pang of disappointment. What had I expected? But yesterday I had heard her sing a song that had put fire in my veins. Then she had lifted the curtain and stood before me a woman of marble. To-day I fain would have seen on her young forehead the crown of sacrifice of which I had been told, whose innocent sublimity had profoundly moved me. I would have liked to see the traces of tears on her young face and its memories in her eyes. Instead of this, by one of those tricks fate loves to play on us, she never appeared to me less . . . intricate, if I may so express myself.

She stepped in lightly, her only laurels the charming coquetry with which she had wound a soft *bashlik*, embroidered and tasselled with gold, low about her hair. Her simple dark costume gave her a peculiarly girlish appearance, and she seemed in excellent spirits, and more engrossed with the practical details of our excursion than with matters of deeper sentiment. I almost hated her for her gayety. Was it possible, I asked myself, that all these things about her could be true! My only consolation was that she wore my lilies at her bosom. But I was so agitated by all that I had heard, and there seemed so little *rapport* between my present mood and her own, that I felt no courage to approach and thank her for this piece of sweet feminine flattery. Just then came a rustle of skirts and sound of voices, and a bevy of pretty women fluttered in, followed by a half-dozen men or so. Suwaroff, Berg, the Princesse Soltikoff, little Madame Wassilii, and others. Just before we took our places in the *troïkas*, Mrs. North managed to whisper a word to me:

"You may be surprised, monsieur, that I should have spoken to you, an entire stranger, on these family matters. We Americans are not prone to be expansive. It is not a national trait, but I did not know what stories you might hear. Mrs. Acton's marriage created much comment at the time. She has not lived in a corner, and the world is very small. I only wished you to know what all may know. You have from the first inspired me with confidence; I hear golden opinions of you; am glad to welcome you to our house. I feel that you will not misjudge me."

I could only press her hand warmly and

thank her for her goodness and her faith in me, assuring her never to give her cause of regret. To myself this seemed suddenly to loom up into a sacred pledge, with responsibilities which made me a trifle uneasy.

I had hardly realized my happiness, when I found Mrs. Acton was beside me. In the narrow vehicles into which the party was somewhat overcrowded we were forced into close proximity. Nothing can ever paint the delirium of that drive. I hardly know what occurred. We stopped at the Ice Palace, and she and I and the others—were there others?—wandered into its cold spaces. I told her the story of the thoughtless courtiers who locked up one of their number, with his bride, to pass the night in its white chambers, and who, in the morning hours, found the prisoners dead and stiff. "I have always thought," I said, "that young man must have been strangely lacking in ardor." Like a child, Mrs. Acton wished to be drawn by the reindeer across the palace grounds, and, reclining on furs on the low sledges, our party was carried about and around this fairy castle. I only know I was forced to hold her once by one of her delicate wrists, for fear she should slip off into the snow-drifts. Afterwards in the *troïka* once more, borne away again, as if into untried regions, untasted sensations, unexplored worlds, away to the Islands, through the windless night. Oh, never-to-be-forgotten excursion!

Coming home late, when the dance, the supper, the music were all over, I almost held her in my arms in the soft balancement of the rushing sleigh. I imagined that I could feel her heart-pulses; I was very careful not to offend, fearful as always of incurring her displeasure. She did not herself know how close she was to me. Once my spur became entangled in her skirt. I stooped with ungloved hand to disentangle it. She had herself taken off her glove to readjust a lock of recreant hair fluttering from beneath her veil I handed her her muff, lost in the movement. Our fingers met, clung one instant together. Can such a shock send forth no responding vibration? Is it possible that what I felt was wholly unshared? I know not, but this I know: twice she placed me beside her in the *troïka.* Only once during that blissful night there fell a shadow between us: as I looked down at her lovely face, framed in its high fur collar, nestling so close to mine, she asked me who I should dance with at the coming ball.

"Mademoiselle Taillefère," I answered, "whom I engaged for the cotillon long before I ever met you, madame."

"Ah!" she said; "I have not seen her. Is she . . . very nice?"

"She does not particularly interest me," I replied.

"Why did you choose her, then?" she continued, with childlike insistence.

"Oh, I don't know," I answered, carelessly. "Probably because she has a beautiful figure."

It was a stupid speech, uttered without thought, for my blood was in my brain. I noticed that she drew away a little, and devoted herself at least twenty minutes to Berg, who sat at her right. I am not conceited by nature, and racked my mind to imagine why she had grown so silent towards me. It was only afterwards, upon reflection, that I thought perhaps she had not liked what I had said. I cursed Mademoiselle Taillefère, my dulness of perception, and the vulgarity of the remark which had lost me a moment of those precious hours. But if it were true that the words really hurt her,—if it were true, if it were true, what a world of ecstasy this has become!

While she leaned towards Berg I looked at her, and I understood well that one might sacrifice everything to be loved by her, to awaken and warm this proud, delicate creature with the fires of passion. For this I felt that one would throw duty, life, nay, honor itself, to the winds. Yes, I, who have lived so long for ambition only, felt as if to possess her for an hour I would follow her like a dog to the ends of the earth, casting my career and my hopes behind me.

After our hands had touched she came back to me, the *geliebte*, but nevertheless there was a subtle change in her attitude towards me, and her manner, which had been once or twice divinely coquettish, was tinged with a fine hauteur. I longed to tell her how much I loved her, but something held me back and paralyzed my tongue, and she was, I thought, tacitly grateful to me for my reserve. At any rate, I shall take an early opportunity to explain to her how I loathe Mademoiselle Taillefère, who is very plain, and even ill-shapen, for so I consider her beside my goddess.

February 1.—My intoxication has fallen! To-night I look into the future. What does it hold? To pass one's life beside such a being, to leave to her delicate tact the management of all social intricacies, to sleep and wake and know one's self so safe, with time for serious work, while she watched near, her voice, her step, her song in one's ears,—what a heaven! Yet something says to me, "She is not for thee." I know that I love her, because I am profoundly miserable. To realize that she is in Petersburg, so near me, and that I cannot always be with her, cannot fall at her feet, cannot hold her in my arms,—what anguish!

I shall see her to-night at the Odoiëffskys' and adore her at a distance; shall see her officially, surrounded by others, by younger, handsomer fellows, these dashing young Russian officers, the pampered darlings of the women, far better fitted than I to touch and fascinate her imagination. How old and weary and *bassané* my face looks near her fair fresh one! The battle-fields have left their traces. Humph! Women love youth. Ah, Daphne, I am to-day only a tired old war-horse, whom it would be a mercy to put out of his pain! Give me the death-thrust, dear, before you leave me! for—you will leave me . . . I feel it. Such bliss as love of yours is not for me. I am too much stained with living, with the smoke of battle and the fires of the world. Your love would be as a stream of pure water in which to lave soiled garments; it would refresh, rejuvenate, purify an unworthy past. When I am near her, youth returns, and romance. I grow pure. I tremble. I could weep. Why has she roused this longing to hold her close, to fold her to myself, if it is never to be gratified? I am devoured with unrest!

The women are jealous of her. This afternoon they gossiped about her over their tea-tables. These women, who have had lovers by the score, dared to criticise my darling! Odoiëffsky, the beast, had tattled of her. He said to her, "I saw you at the opera, madame."

"Yes," she had replied, "I observed it."

"I am desolated, madame, if my admiration of you was too pronounced, if I looked at you too constantly."

"Oh, pray don't distress yourself, monsieur," she had replied. "It is quite unnecessary. That is what I go out for."

Everybody was shocked. The men winked at one another and shrugged their shoulders. The women exclaimed, "*Les Américaines sont à un tel point mal élevées!* What! they are without shame!" and rolled up their eyes, duly scandalized, until the whites appeared.

A shrill voice came to the rescue.

"Who knows? Perhaps it was exaggerated.

She might not have said such a thing. If she did it was certainly *atroce*."

But I knew that she had said it, because it was exactly like her, angel that she is, and a flood of passionate loyalty rose to my lips, and a flush overspread my entire face, for which I cursed myself inwardly.

"Do you think that she really said it?" persisted the last speaker, turning to me. "You know her very well, I believe?"

"Yes," I replied, "I am sure that she did, madame, and it would be as difficult to defend her as it is impossible to imitate her."

There was an embarrassing moment of silence, for my tone had a ring that the ladies did not relish. There was a murmur, and some dagger-glances.

"Men admire these oddities," said Madame Wassilii, with elevated eyebrow.

"Yes, madame, they do, for to be with an enchantress like Mrs. Acton is as if one should turn from listening to the screaming chatter of little tame popinjays to watch the evolutions of some splendid wild white sea-bird."

"Ah! *il est pris!*" cried the women, in sharp concerto. "*Pincé!*" And I became the target for their pitiless raillery, not untinged with resentment.

I did manage with certain artifices of gallantry, not unnecessarily learned in my career, to patch up some sort of a peace with my persecutors, and to extricate myself from an awkward position. I had shown too much heat, and had been perhaps unwise. I marvelled at the temerity with which I had spoken, but had I not done so I should have suffocated. Daphne is original; it is a crime that her sex never pardons.

A splendid ball at the Odoiëffskys', utterly wretched to me, for . . . she did not come. People said it was a brilliant affair. Madame Odoiëffsky in white velvet, and resplendent with all her diamonds; Odoiëffsky himself very handsome in his Cossack uniform, with its cartridge case of *niello* silver at his belt. I could have throttled him for having babbled of Daphne. Sitting on the stairs, amid all the throng of gay people, was the little paralyzed son of the house, his rich velvet dress and white lace ruffles contrasting strangely with his poor pinched face, the lips drawn away on one side from the teeth in that terrible set smile. They have grown accustomed to him. They do not realize how he appears to strangers. His big bony head, with its scant hair and livid skin, prominent nose, and beautiful, lustrous eyes, full of a sort of restless pathos, set upon attenuated little shoulders, filled me with sympathy and pain. They grant him all his whims, and he had insisted on seeing the ball from this particular perch. Elegant women leaned lightly to him, and threw him a smile as they passed up and down, inwardly shuddering, and thanking God for their ruddy little ones at home.

As the ball grew, however, and after the Mazurka began, little Feodor was almost forgotten. I thought that he and I were the most lonely and miserable people present, for I had grown half-sick with waiting. So I carried the child some sweets from the supper, and I showed him my sword, and I explained and told him stories about all of my decorations. The only moments of peace that I found were at the side of this unfortunate boy. The pity that I felt for his misfortunes seemed to alleviate my own suffering.

Life holds three phases,—that of hope, that of revolt, and that of philosophy. I have reached the age of the latter, but it is not yet fully my own. Why did she not come? and what is she? A woman worthy of my adoration, or a cold coquette, playing with me for her amusement? What is she? I must know, and she shall tell me herself, yes, to-morrow! Perhaps then I shall not feel so separated from her, so far. What long years behind us both we wot not of! She looks to me like a woman of inexorable will. How much of mine would it need to win her? Ah, I would not hurt you, dear! One feels that love is her essence. Ariadne's thread would guide her step by step through the obscure labyrinths in which I would soon lose my way and my reason. The sensibilities of these frail creatures are more quick than ours, but are they as profound?

What breaks and mars a man's heart passes over a woman's like a breeze of spring-time. It is easy to shake the dew from a rose, but the old oak's bark must be torn and broken to give out a drop of the sap which lends it force.

February 2.—I have seen her alone, and we have had a serious explanation, or, rather, I poured out myself and told her something of my own past. Later I begged her to talk to me of her own life.

"My own life was too much bound up with that of others," she said. "I cannot speak of it."

"What must you think of me, then," I said, "who have bared so much of my soul to you? Have I been too frank?"

"Ah, that would be so nice," she said, playfully, "to find that you could be indiscreet or unwise, for they say you are so clever and strong. I am a true woman, and it would be delicious to me to find a weak spot in my knight's armor."

That is all the comfort I got.

"Ah!" I said; "the tears which fell from

your eyes the other day were more eloquent than any words those mobile lips can speak."

Then she admitted shyly, like a young girl, that the only *man* she had met was . . . myself. I fell at her feet; she bade me rise, and said, "What folly!" but she did not send me away. She is a most fascinating woman.

February 3.—I have always thought I should like to bear away with me to Italy the woman I loved; to have her near me under hot and sunny skies, my beloved, my *fiancée*, or my bride. It is true the thought of marriage has not largely occupied my horizons! I have always hated these cold countries. Why, then, does their mysterious melancholy seem to suit and melt into my present mood and the *farouche* nature of my love for her? I am glad that I have known her here. I would like to carry Daphne away, wrapped against my bosom, to the granite-bound lakes of Finland, to drink in by her side the acrid odors of the pines, or, farther away still, to the sombre steppes of Orenbourg; into some dim region where the strife of tongues should have ceased, and where she alone would be my warmth and my sunlight. With such a one as she, one would want space and solitude.

"*Enfin ils trouvèrent un vaste champ où on était à l'aise et en liberté!*"

I remember Borodino, and that long, dusty road to Smolensk, through which Napoleon passed, leaving devastation behind him,—that theatre of glory and of bloody exploits. I was there once, a traveller and sight-seer, wasting a few days' furlough on my way to Bucharest. I stopped at the monastery Siemienoffskaia, and rested one warm June night by the river Kolotcha. Why do I think of that night now? I sat on the shore watching the anxious turbid green waters. I was alone. All was forgotten,—the rush of the troops, the cries of victorious armies. How still it was! Like death, like an early death, on that vast plain, the tomb of thousands. There was no stir in the dumb silence except that of the winds through the sad willows and scraggy lindens, waking a distant echo of the great epic of the century. Why this memory now? and why would I like to carry my Daphne away with me to the quiet shores of the river Kolotcha, where none could follow us?

Daphne! What a sweet perfume about that name! What a pretty name! I never could make a D when I was a child. It is certainly a difficult letter. Bah! I am getting into my dotage.

February 9.—How could I write anything? I have seen her constantly. I must collect my thoughts of her. They press so tumultuously. After I last wrote we visited one afternoon the little Palace of Peter the Great, the Zoo, and the Church of St. Paul and St. Peter Citadel, mausoleum of the Czars. We were a *partie carrée*, the Princesse Soltikoff and Berg.

How graceful she looked, how radiant; how tranquil and elegant her movements, how noble the poise of her small head! She was delighted with the quaint little toy house and its big sentries. Sitting opposite to her in Madame Soltikoff's carriage,—it was too bitterly cold for our sleighs,—I was myself as happy as a school-boy. I leaned over several times and whispered to her, "I love you!" She blushed, and once she returned my glance. As I said before, to those who have never met the gaze of this woman it would be impossible to explain its power. The eye is long, light, half-closed, not very brilliant or of decided hue. It is neither blue nor black nor green nor gray, its interior emotions alone seeming to make it glitter or pale. Its habitual expression is one of indifference, or of impenetrable coldness, when it shrouds its fires. But if it allow but a spark to escape, how shall one paint the voluptuousness of its expression or the pang that it pours into a man's being? One becomes her slave, however mistrustfully. Would any man dare to marry a woman with such eyes?

Her mouth, tempting and luscious, is more telltale. She has a way of leaning back with half-open lips. It is quite impossible that she realizes the effect. It would be a cruelty.

At the Zoo we made the acquaintance of

monsieur and madame and the little hippopotamus. Also we met some members of the Chinese legation, whose eyeballs and pigtails seemed to tremble with pleasure when they saw our fair companions. We were a merry party, all but Berg, who is hopelessly *épris* of Madame Acton, and does me the honor to be jealous. Returning, we dismissed the carriage at the bridge, and all walked home together across the Néva through the snow, and thence skirting the *quais* into the *Lietné Sadou.* We wandered aimlessly for a while in its dim alleys. All I knew was that I was near her.

It is tacitly accepted now between us that I am devoted to her, and that there are to be no further explanations at present; that we are to drift for a while wherever the winds of fate and her wishes shall waft us. She desires this.

"Don't let us become tragic," she said to me. "I rest upon your honor not to speak of your love to me,—not just now, not just now,—later, later. Let us enjoy these hours innocently and carelessly like children."

She seems to dread any decision or any avowal. Shall I admit that there is a certain charm in the vagueness of the situation, which certainly cannot prolong itself for many weeks. It is a curious fact that this woman inspires me with such timidity, such fear of losing her altogether, that I obey.

February 10.—Her conversation interests me deeply. We were speaking of excursions in the mountains of Switzerland the other day, and she alluded to a trip she had taken into the hills of her own country. "I hate mountains," she said, "except in the distance. It is not that I lack the courage to scale them. In fact," she added, "I have so much of that quality that I have sometimes wondered if it were not effrontery."

I made a gesture in deprecation.

"Oh, I know!" she continued, wilfully misunderstanding me. "It is not a virtue that commends one to the gentlemen. Well, *à propos* of the mountains, I am not lazy nor timid, but I only want to look up at them; at the calm majesty of their summits where they mingle with the eternal skies. I have always thought they were just like great people, marred and disfigured, when you approach them, by sticks and stumps and ugly stones over which one trips and falls and hurts one's self. Madame de Rémusat went mountaineering when she gossiped about Napoleon's weaknesses. Ah me! it is only to very superior minds we dare show our weakness. Little people like Madame de Rémusat can only dwell upon the trifles. They harp on the irregularities and the defects, and they jump at conclusions about people's tone of mind and generally unsound *morale* on slight and dubious evidences."

Another time I spoke in scorn of wealth. "Ah, my friend," she said, "money means freedom, and freedom is power." Talking of early youth, one day, she said, "Youth is the period of disappointments, and suffers tortures through the fear of ridicule. It dies in sublime silence rather than face adverse criticisms. We," she added, laughingly, "my friend, are at the best and happiest age."

"We?" I replied. "You are sarcastic, madame. Why, I am old enough to be your father."

"You must have been very precocious, then, for I really am a very old person."

"Well preserved," I replied, smiling.

"Oh, yes, nice-looking enough; but I assure you plain people have one incalculable advantage in that they never vary, and one always knows exactly where to find them, whereas the handsome ones manage at times to look surprisingly hideous."

She rose and walked to the mirror and contemplated herself for a moment, lifting the hair a little which grows low on her young forehead,—that proud forehead upon which one unconsciously looks for a diadem.

"Do you think me handsome?" she said, suddenly, turning and facing me.

"Yes."

"There are quantities of things all wrong, you know."

i

"Yes, I have remarked it. Nature has been indeed most niggardly, and I pity you for your unfortunate appearance and myself for my bad taste."

"My husband, Mr. Acton, used to say there was no real beauty, only a very good . . . effect."

The words seemed to escape her involuntarily. It was the first time she had ever mentioned her husband to me. I grew silent.

"How stern your face becomes at times," she said, laughing. "You look ready to commit some dreadful crime."

She can jest with a dead man's name on her lips, I thought to myself, with a sudden pain. Has she no heart? And yet her lips are full of fascination and of truth.

February 12.—By appointment I walked this morning in the *Lietné Sadou* with Mrs. Acton. "Take me for a walk!" she had said to me the day before. I dismissed my sleigh at the gate and entered between the sentinels. The alleys were deserted except for the distant bent figure of Gen. Z., who exercises his old blind dog here every morning, the only dog ever admitted into these quiet precincts.

"What will you have?" the Czar asked of the gallant officer, when he came back covered with glory from his battle-fields.

"Your Majesty," he replied, "don't separate me from my faithful Sachs when I take my walk every morning in the Summer Garden."

"Your wish shall be a law," said the grateful sovereign, so every day at eleven precisely the sentries salute the master and his decrepit companion.

The guns from the fortress were popping away in commemoration, no doubt, of some *fête* day I knew nothing about. To my ear there is always something peculiarly exhilarating in the sound of artillery, albeit this was somewhat too distant to whip up my blood to pleasant heat. But woman takes the place of battle in my to-day, and the delicious expectation of her kept me warm in the biting air. In a moment I heard her footstep crunching the snow, and bright with the morning she stood before me under the bare white trees.

"I sent the sleigh and chasseur to the *quais*," she said, "so we have plenty of time to explore this charming place. Oh, monsieur, I love it!"

I kissed her gloved hand, drawn a moment from her great muff. It is a strong hand. I dreamed last night I was holding her hands against my breast. They felt so cool. The points of the fingers seemed to be wandering over my heart. When I awoke I was conscious of a peculiar delightful physical sensation, a *bien-être*, which has clung to me ever since. It was a sweet dream. God! how beautiful women are!

To return to Daphne. We had not walked many steps when Miss Xavier and her maid loomed suddenly before us. She bowed, staring a little with her near-sighted eyes. A few rods farther we crossed the path of the Princesse Soltikoff's young daughter Dina and her governess. The child was rosy and happy; she skipped and capered about on the unshovelled snow-drifts which were piled up against the mysterious forms of the covered statues. Full of animal spirits, she called out after me, "*Monsieur, monsieur, quand venez-vous patiner avec moi à la Tauride?* Come Thursday! Come Thursday! There will be a quadrille on the ice, music, and I am going to dance!"

The governess muttered a hasty excuse and reproved her charge sharply for *inconvenance*, seizing her roughly by the shoulders, over which hung a quantity of rich auburn curls.

"Why, what has the poor little thing done that was so dreadful?" asked Mrs. Acton.

"Addressed a man first, before he spoke to her," I replied.

"Since when has that been criminal?"

"Young girls here are kept very strictly."

"She is a pretty child. The Princess has not yet shown me her children."

"Are you fond of children?"

"No, I dislike them. But I do love very much one little child."

"And what little child is that?"

"My sister's boy."

"Happy little boy!"

After a short silence she said to me, reflectively, "Am I indiscreet to walk with you here alone?"

"If you were a resident, possibly. Being a stranger and a traveller, much is overlooked." I was going to say "an American," but fortunately checked myself.

"Ah!" Mrs. Acton grew a little haughty.

"This is of course a perfectly proper place for a promenade,—the most elegant, in fact, which Petersburg offers. Believe me I should never have engaged you to do anything compromising."

"Compromising!"

Shall I admit the exclamation was not uttered quite gently? "Fancy," she added, after a moment's pause, "my doing anything . . compromising!"

I felt we were treading on dangerous ground and hastened to distract her thoughts. "You came promptly, and I want to tell you how much I admire you for this. Some women seem to think that to keep a man hanging about for an hour in Siberian winter weather adds to their attractions. If they only knew men better! But you, my fair American princess, have no need of such vulgar arts. You arrive when you promise, tranquil and fresh, with no excuse on your lips, or hurry in your gait. So must goddesses have come when they descended to mortals. Where have you learned what a man likes best?"

"I have always dared to be . . . myself," she answered, with evident pleasure at my flattery.

"And who and what are you?"

"Ah! that too is mine to keep. Why . . . do you ever think ill of me?"

"Sometimes."

"And what do you think?"

"Before I reply to that question much more time must be given me to ponder the riddle that you are."

"Am I a riddle? That delights me."

"Yes, and I must not only solve it, but I must find out too what the riddle thinks of me; where I stand."

"That I shall not divulge."

"Yet you have come no doubt to some conclusions about me?"

"To all."

"Your opinion is made up?"

"Absolutely."

"And you leave me in darkness?"

"Quite."

"Is that kind?"

"Perhaps."

"Ah!" I said, sadly, "you have betrayed yourself. I know now I do not stand well in your estimation."

We had approached the little tea-house of the late Czar, where he used to come and drink fragrant *chay*, and rest, away from labors of state and boresome etiquette. Who knows? to chat perhaps with the woman who for so many years ruled his fate. It was now melancholy and deserted. The royal servants who are delegated to keep it always as it was in the days of its august owner were either asleep or neglectful. The rooms, as far as we could see through the thick coating of ice which encrusted the windows, were deserted, empty, and forlorn. Daphne placed her lips to one of the panes and breathed upon it to melt the frost. " I want to look in," she said.

I am afraid I seized this opportunity to stand very close to her, our *shubas* touching each other, my sword against her skirts. She gave a little low cry. "Oh, but it is cold!" she said, and drew back quickly. I approached my own lips to drink in, with strange avidity, what perfume might remain of her breath upon the icy glass. It seemed to my fancy still hot from her contact. A vertigo seized me. I reeled slightly and covered my eyes for a moment with one of my hands. When I recovered my reason she was looking at me fixedly; her face was pale.

"My friend," she said, "you asked me just now how you stood with me. Some day I will tell you, but not now, not now. I implore you, I implore you, let us be happy a few short hours, a few short days, and let the—let the—" she faltered a moment—"let the flesh be in abeyance. Of it are born all love's woes, exactions, tyrannies, jealousies. Stifle it, stifle it, and forgive the evil in me which temnts you!"

She held out her hand to me with a sweet womanly gesture, so frank and appealing that I could not doubt its sincerity. I folded it warmly in my own.

"Angel or sorceress," I said, "it is not you, then, that I will try to vanquish, but myself You tell me nothing, you vaguely hint at some barrier between us; if it be, as I believe, of your own making, you alone can remove it. I will bide your own time, I will be patient, yet do not try me too far, for I am only a man after all."

She looked at me gratefully. "This is a compact, then?" she said, more lightly.

I tried after this to keep within the bounds of strict reserve, but I must confess the task rather overtops my powers. At the *quais* we met the sleigh and Alexei, but it was still early, and Madame Acton declared that she enjoyed the exercise and would prefer to walk home.

An incident occurred during this homeward walk which struck me disagreeably. Before fully realizing the fact I found we were approaching the famous yacht club. I suggested to Mrs. Acton the propriety of taking some other street or retracing our steps.

"I cannot imagine why," she said.

"It is an unpleasant areopagus for a lady to pass. All the diplomatic corps and young guardsmen are there in the morning, and you will not like to run the blockade of their silly and often indecent jests."

"Indecent!" She said it in a good deal the same tone with which she had uttered the one word "compromising," and a certain hardness came over her fair visage. "I think I can stand these gentlemen," she continued. "My actions can bear the light. Come, *mon ami*, we will not retreat before the enemy!"

"As you like," I replied, a little coldly, for I was secretly vexed at what I considered a piece of childish obstinacy. The words were hardly uttered before a party of young men, talking loudly and smoking their cigarettes, came striding forth from out of the club. The sidewalk was encumbered with some boxes, over which a couple of tradesmen were disputing with many Russian expletives, and these young officers had to scatter to let me and my companion pass. In fact, for a moment we were surrounded by them. Men of fashion of our time are not remarkable either for their timidity or their chivalry. Those whom I knew gave me a military salute. One or two had met or seen Mrs. Acton, and bowed low as she passed with her usual easy grace. A good deal of bold staring was indulged in, however, and I heard "*Tiens! a-t-il de la chance avec sa jolie Américaine, le malin!*"

"*Il nous devance, mon cher.*"

Extremely annoyed, I hurried to join Mrs. Acton, expecting to see displeasure depicted upon her face. Imagine my surprise when I only found there an expression of great satisfaction. "I said I would do it," she cried, exultingly. "Wasn't it amusing?"

"It is a form of amusement, madame, which I confess does not commend itself to my taste," I replied, stiffly.

"They were so surprised to see you with

me," she continued, entirely ignoring my vexation. "What do you suppose they thought? What did they say? I could not hear."

The devil take me if I tell her, I muttered to myself, inwardly. "They said it was a very cold day: only four degrees," I replied, laconically.

"Why are you so cross to me? I was just beginning to enjoy myself;" and I noticed the color had indeed returned to Daphne's lips and cheeks, and that there was a feverish animation in her usually half-shut, dreamy eyes. Shall I admit that I was forced to conclude that this lady of my adoration, this angel at whose feet I was ready to cast myself down at the sacrifice of all my dignity and all my manhood, had found a diabolical delight in dragging me, the "impregnable," conspicuously about, and parading me tied hand and foot to her skirts past a club which is the hot-bed of all Petersburg scandals, and this a few moments only after a scene of such fine delicacy and tender romance as had been enacted between us amid the snows of the *Lietné Sadou?*

While I was indulging in these reflections she dismissed me abruptly, saying, "You seem morose. I will leave you now. I prefer to finish my walk alone," and did in fact leave me planted upon the sidewalk. I groaned to myself as I stumbled home, utterly wretched, after this abrupt farewell, for, the club exploit over, Daphne seemed to have no further use for me, and to have become quickly weary of my society. It is certain and decided that she is without heart. Has she not admitted to me that she hates children? It is also certain that she has no discretion, that even her taste and delicacy are at fault, and that . . . I adore her!

February 13.—How could I so malign her! She is all heart, all taste, all delicacy, all discretion, only she is *très femme*, which means full of contradictions that no blundering man can ever understand. It is conclusive that she enjoyed passing that club. I saw every evidence of it. But why? Was it vanity? A little, perhaps, and the purity which does not know how wicked these men's tongues can be, the fools—would that I might cut their tongues out for them! But I have not the right to mix up Mrs. Acton's name in any brawl, and this would be the only and sure result. I can trust to my natural reserve and dignity to stop the slightest further allusion to our matutinal ramble, only . . . she must be more prudent. People here will not comprehend. I have heard that the Americans trust their women implicitly and accord them extraordinary liberty. In theory I believe them to be right; personally I confess that the Sultan's method of lock and key would suit me better, for I will confide to my journal, and to my journal alone, that I am of an intensely jealous disposition, and do not possess that faith which makes existence so delightfully calm. Call it trust, if you will; I name it conceit.

February 15 was perhaps one of the dreariest days I ever spent. I noticed that the extreme unctuousness and marked courtesies which have characterized the attitude of this government's high officials towards my humble person seemed to have received a sudden check. The Czar, to be sure, extended friendly finger-tips, but the gentlewomen of the Empress's *entourage*, and this lovely lady herself, were barely polite, while at the foreign office there was, as it were, a smell of gunpowder in the air. Later I learned of the violent political and personal attack upon me in the *Moscow Gazette*, which I had not seen earlier in the day. Before evening I had taken steps to prosecute its editor. However vexing a *procès* and its publicity is to me at this moment, the world shall vindicate me, and these proud people shall be brought to terms. I owe it to the government I serve as well as to my own self-respect. What! I am to be treated as a spy! I, whose every instinct rebels against crooked or tortuous means! My fault has been too much bluntness, too much honesty—never too little. Rather to my amusement, I found myself deluged by telegrams from friends, all of course kindly offering advice or aid.

I clipped the attack and sent it to Mrs. Acton, with a word asking her if she believed these vile stories of one whom she honored with her friendship. August brought me back her answer: "I will meet you at the Tauride to morrow and will confer on this matter with you. I am too American, you know, to do anything but laugh at the attacks of the press, which with us has not liberty, but license. I know here, however, such matters are more grave, and particularly to one in your delicate position. But, *mon ami, I believe in you.*" That was all. Oh, angel!

Harassed by the annoyance of running about for counsel and getting into shape for my *procès*, I came home to find some necessary papers. Gustav, who opened the door for me, drew me aside as I entered, with a most mysterious expression of countenance. "Your Excellency," he said, "indeed I said you were out; I even lied and said *il découche*, but in she came and in she would remain. She asked for a glass of vodka, your Excellency, and she emptied it so,—as a child would its milk;" and Gustav tossed off an imaginary draught and smacked his lips with a noisy cluck.

"*Va à tous les diables!*" I hurled at him. Inwardly enraged, I entered my rooms, to find

Madame Nathalie in full possession. "I thought you were gone," I said, inhospitably, albeit advancing to salute her. "Surely your engagement at the 'Marie' is over?"

"*Mon cher*, you see I am not," she said, "since I come in for a chat with you."

"It will have to be short," I answered, curtly. "I am very busy."

"Oh yes, I knew you were in trouble, but there are things even more terrible than a false accusation."

I did not care to discuss my affairs with the importunate danseuse, but something in her tone was so *triste* and earnest that I involuntarily unbent a little. Smoothing the wrinkles out of my nose, which is the feature upon which my brother says that all my displeasure concentrates, I handed her a cigarette, lighted my own pipe, and asked her a little more good humoredly what the matter was.

"It is just this," she said, leaning back in a low chair, and exhibiting a pair of tightly-fitting dark-blue hose. In my newly-assumed character of Joseph I blinked and turned away, laughing at myself a little in my sleeve at the same time.

Why is it that play-actresses are always at their *rôle?* they never can be sincere for three minutes consecutively. When she saw I meant to be more civil the mima was all alive again.

"You can prevent a . . . murder," she cried, tragically.

"It is so difficult, my fair one, to know if you are telling the truth, fabricating something for your own amusement, or simply——"

She interrupted me with a violent gesture. "Listen to me," she said, "for a moment," and this time there was a return of truthfulness in the ring of her voice. "I may be a fool, but you owe me something."

"I will not interrupt you again."

"You remember the night you took me away from the little Frenchman's insolence at the guardsmen's supper. Well, who else would have done it? You knew, all Petersburg knew, what my relations had been with S., and that I had been under his protection for nearly two years. Yes, let me see." She counted rapidly on her fingers. "I don't allude to three months in Italy," she murmured, as if in doubt as to who had protected her during those. "Well, long before that night it was all over between us. We were *bons camarades.* His love for me was quite dead, quite, and you yourself saw how coldly he stood by and heard that boy insult me. Well, will you believe it? since that evening when you,—when he saw how much I liked you, and the fellows have called you my protector, —ever since then his feeling for me seems to have reawakened. He never cared about d'Aubilly; he only laughed, for, as I tell you, it was all up between us. But now, now, he swears if I don't come back to him he will kill himself. He is half wild, he is drinking dreadfully. He frightens me. He says he will shoot you too the next time you come to the Michel riding-school, or at the first carousal of the Chevalier Guardsmen, as if you were a dog of a Kirgheez. I don't think he will kill you; he would not dare. He knows what I would do to him then. But I think he is or will be killing himself." She stopped, breathless.

"And what am I to do about it?"

"Go and see him and tell him there is nothing between us. Calm his jealousy. He is like an insane child."

"Why should I go on such a fool's errand? Have you not told him that yourself?"

"Yes, but he only curses me and says it is a lie; says he knows I love you, and you see, *mon cher*," she added, and a tear, yes, an actual tear, rolled down her cheek, bringing with it a little streak of rouge, "the fact is that . . . I think I am *amoureuse pour de bon* this time."

"We are not here to discuss your sentiments, madame," I said, flicking the ashes from my pipe. "But you yourself admit the man has ceased to love you; then why, in heaven's name, should he care a kopeck who you give yourself to or whom you honor with your . . . affections?"

"Passion outlives love," said Nathalie.

"Humph! You have cracked a nut there in whose kernel lies a grain of truth. I see that you study psychology as well as vertiginous *entrechats.*"

Delighted to have arrested my interest for a moment, my tormentor was not slow in profiting by her advantage. "But I would rather die on the straw than go back to S. It was a dog's life that he led me. When he was jealous he used to pull my hair out, yes, by the roots." She put up her hands in illustration of this picturesque confession, and gave a hard jerk to a handful of her crisp, thick hair, which seemed to resist fairly well this demand upon its powers of resistance. "But you, but you, how kind you could be to a woman, how gentle and how tender! Tell me, Monsieur le Comte, why am I repulsive to you?"

She rose and came close to me. A very pretty woman certainly is Madame Nathalie. Superb are her ripe charms, and I could feel her breath close to my face and see the small cruel teeth glisten between the dry parted lips, but God is my witness that fiom her panting bosom not a spark flashed to my own, and that before this magnificent creature offering herself to me so impudently in the face of the danger to her former lover, which she seemed sincere in believing, I remained as cold as marble.

"What did you come here for?" I said to her, savagely. "Was it to save a suicide or to tempt a cynic?"

She looked at me a moment very strangely. Her eyes grew big and black and her face blanched under its cosmetics.

"Who is it? I will know, I will know!" she said, under her breath. "If it is a *femme du monde* she shall eat the dust."

Tragics usually produce in me a nervous impulse of laughter, and I indulged now in a guffaw which was calculated to clear like thunder the electrical atmosphere. She shrank and seemed to feel that she had been ridiculous, which piqued her vanity as a woman of the world.

"You only laugh," she muttered, a little ashamed. "Only tell me if the woman you care for is a *femme du monde*, then I will leave you, will never trouble you again?"

"Yes," I said. "Now go!"

"Is she *Russkaia?*" she persisted.

"I insist that this scene shall end!"

"What do you advise me about Strogonoff?"

"Go back to him."

"What! you whom I adore would drive me back to the arms of the man I hate?"

"Go to the devil, both of you, only leave me in peace now and hereafter!" I cried.

"You will be sorry for this," she said, in a stifled key.

Somehow the woman managed to make me uneasy, and I weakly compromised by helping her into her shuba and accompanying her to the door.

The antechamber once cleared of her presence and her essences, I collared Gustav and gave him such a shaking as I will wager he never had had before in his experiences as a valet. "Take that, and remember it," I said; "and I will break your bones and not pay the doctor who sets them if ever you let that jade into my rooms again! Did you take her money, you dog?"

"*Na, gnädige Herr*, I would not touch the lady's money, and you are too violent," mumbled Gustav; and then he called out after me, "*Na, gnädige Herr*, but she is a fine woman for all that, but when the court ladies smile on a man he loses his head, and does not know his real friends from enemies that shall bring him to dishonor."

The exact portent of my angry servant's tirade I did not stop to fathom, but I was left with a sense of *malaise*. I had been brutal to a woman, I had ill used a faithful domestic, and I had an unpleasant sense that Daphne might come to some harm through this woman's machinations. Whence come to us these premonitions? Certain it is that the disaster which followed my inaction and its remorse will linger with me long.

Two hours later I was lounging on the quay, hoping that the Norths' sleigh, with a certain wished-for figure hidden among its furs, might pass me, when a man ran wildly out of a house and almost fell against me. "Ah, monsieur," he said, in French, "God sent you! My poor master! my poor master! He is dead! Come in! come in! For God's sake, come and help us!" His manner was so agonized and vehement that a crowd began to gather about us. I seized his arm and pushed him into the house.

I recognized him at once as Strogonoff's servant, having seen him waiting at his master's supper-table, and again in attendance upon him at the opera.

"What has happened?" I said, huskily, stepping into the door-way which led to Strogonoff's apartments. The other servants were gathered in the hall, full of dismay and consternation.

"Quick, Piotre, go for a doctor!" some one cried, and then,—"Wait! we must telegraph at once to Varinka Nicolaevna, at Nice!"

The Princesse Varinka was Strogonoff's married sister, and his only near relative.

In the general confusion I found myself led into the unfortunate young man's rooms, which were upon the ground floor. "This way, this way, and for God's sake help us!" wailed the unhappy valet.

I ordered two of the servants away, one for a physician, and one with the telegram, and myself entered Strogonoff's bedroom with his body servant, the Frenchman Léon, who had met me in the street. He lay as they had found him, face downward. His powerful frame was still clad in his full-dress uniform, his gold-embroidered white dolman hung limp from one of his shoulders; he had on his boots. The early Russian twilight had closed in, but the room would have been dark in any case, for the curtains were carefully drawn, and only two wax-candles burned upon the table. Between them, and close to the sofa where the dying man lay, was a photograph in a jewelled frame. The lights fell full upon its pale surface, while the rest of the great high-ceilinged room was in almost entire obscurity. I noticed even in this dreadful moment, with the insistence with which details force themselves upon an excited mind, that it was a portrait of Nathalie in her *rôle* of Sieba. It was a fine photograph and a flattered likeness, with a daring, saucy glance in the bright eyes.

As I turned the poor boy over in my arms I groaned over the depths of human folly. He was breathing still. A red stream dripped from between his lips. "Blood, blood," moaned Léon, wringing his hands. "My poor master!" I placed my handkerchief close to his mouth, then motioned Léon to approach a light. "It is not blood," I said. "It is red wine. The lungs are intact. The ball has entered his side, and he is vomiting. This is from the stomach."

"Ay, wine, wine and cards, and that woman," said Léon. "He has been a foolish fellow, sir, and it has brought him to this." The man seemed fond of his master; he was weeping.

We were undressing him when the doctors arrived. Thèrémin thinks the wound not necessarily fatal. Later came a telegram from the Princess: "I take midnight train. If he still lives tell him I will pay all debts. Varinka Z."

But Strogonoff continued unconscious, and no such comforting assurance could reach his deaf ears. I went home broken and tired. I hardly have had time to reflect a moment on the extraordinary coincidences of this wretched day and night.

February 17.—The ball had entered the stomach; it could not be extracted. He expired on the following night. I have been much affected by this death. Yet what could I have done?

February 20, *Bezdany, Lithuanie.*—I have been forced to travel here to procure an important witness for my lawsuit. I welcomed the opportunity thus afforded me to escape for a few days from Petersburg, and to shake off the painful impressions which I found it well-nigh impossible to dispel. I am all the more reconciled to this brief absence from the fact that my American friends have gone into Finland for a short excursion. Here my old friend Serge Oussoff, whom I knew in Paris four years since, has offered me the hospitality of his country home, and here I am very comfortably established for two or three days. He told me I must furnish myself with a gun, hunting-knife, furred boots and vest, as he wished me during my sojourn to participate in a bear-hunt. These lords of the Russian forests are not rare in the great wastes of pine which skirt the environs of Wilna.

Oussoff himself met me at the station, and while we drank a glass of beer in its murky restaurant he ordered his man Lachevitch to tell us a bear-story for my especial benefit. Taking off his greasy cap, coughing and spitting first, as do all moujiks on important occasions, Lachevitch began to relate his late experiences in the woods. I understood perfectly well that this was to whet my appetite for personal exploit, and the tale was sufficiently highly colored and incredible to awaken the ardor of the most languid sportsman. At any rate, the man himself, apart from his hunter's boastfulness, was delightfully picturesque. When he had finally killed and cut up his bear, he blew his nose between his thumb and index finger, and proceeded to wipe these digits upon his *touloup.* "Most people," he said, addressing the nondescript hangers-on who had drawn around us, "prefer tracking rabbits to killing bears; it is more familiar;" at which everybody laughed immoderately.

We drove ten versts in the sleigh to Serge's house, which is presided over by an old *gouvernante,* Madame Krioukoff. She gave us some breakfast as soon as we arrived. As she poured out our *chay* from the great silver samovar she expatiated on the fearful dangers of bear-hunting, saying that the animals were thick-hided, and that if one missed them, or, worse still, only wounded them, they would tear a man's cranium open and play with his jaw-bones. She shook her head dolefully from side to side until the little curls of her yellow wig trembled. For her part, she thought "partridges much better game; better to eat, too, and easier to bring home."

Serge only replied, "You chatter too much, you chatter too much, Masha Yacovlena," which reproof the old lady accepted good-humoredly, as if she regarded it rather in the light of flattery. After breakfast my special guide was brought in and presented to me, or rather I was put under his care. They called him Nico. An icon was suspended in the sitting-room where we had assembled after the meal. A light burned before it. Before Nico undertook his new duties he passed fully ten minutes at prayer before this image, making innumerable signs of the cross and balancing his body backward and forward on his heels. He was a short man with heavy shoulders, oldish, with a long white beard. He wore a touloup which looked as if it had served for coat, mattress, napkin, and handkerchief, yet I dare say it will be a part of his eldest son's inheritance.

Having put himself right with heaven, he greeted me respectfully and deigned to take an interest in me. I told him I had never hunted the bear, and that the only live ones I had ever seen were in the zoological gardens of great cities, or led by Italian organ-grinders. "That," he replied, gravely and politely, "is hardly sufficient." The moujik is always civil. He has even tact on occasions, and this one concealed the scorn he must have felt for me with a *savoir-faire* which would have done credit to a courtier.

It was concluded, as my stay was to be so short, that we should start very early the next day. We did, in fact, start at three o'clock. Oussoff himself came into my room on tiptoe with a lamp in his hand, and told me I must hurry, as the *troïka* would be there in twenty minutes. I had slept badly, and felt a good deal like a man who is awakened for his execution. In the *troïka* we found stowed away, besides our arms, several bottles of wine and of brandy. It was snowing and windy. The coachman tossed up his reins, gave a low whistle, and off we swept, leaving behind us two deep ruts in the white surface of the road. "Go on, my little darlings," he cried to his horses, and we did indeed "go on." It was a frantic pace. After a while we pulled up before a miserable hut which seemed to loom up suddenly in the mist.

"Here we are!" cried Serge. It was Nico's abode. On entering I was almost choked by an atmosphere which it is impossible to describe, —an odor of grease, smoke, old sheepskins and unwashed humanity. The family had not yet arisen. They seemed to be asleep all over the floor. "Come, get up!" ordered their master. In a moment every one was on his or her legs; the women began to tie up their hair, the children to whimper, and the men to pray before the sacred images. It was a most extraordinary scene. All these people seemed to have slept in their clothes. I expressed my amazement to Serge, who only shrugged his shoulders. "What will you have? It is a wonder the cow and the pig are not in here too." And this was all the explanation he vouchsafed. Nico was drawing on his boots and looking after his rusty old gun. He handled it tenderly and with a sort of respect, running its bayonet slowly up and down his thumb.

Two men now loomed up at the door-way: one was called Isoph, the other seemed to be nameless. I could hardly distinguish their peasant faces. They seemed younger than Nico, but not more alert. They whispered something to him, and he answered, "Directly." He then detained us a moment longer while he performed his early orisons, after which he saluted everybody very politely. "There is a bear at two versts from here," he said as we sallied out into the snow, "and I think we hold him." A party of moujiks awaited us outside. They were mostly, Serge told me, Nico's sons and sons-in-law. It was still snowing softly, but the wind had blown itself out.

Our *troïka* drew up on the outskirts of the woods and we alighted. We all walked half a mile in silence. It was a painful march, for the snow was up to our knees. Suddenly Nico stopped. "Do you see that mound of snow surmounted by a sort of vapor?" he whispered. We stopped and saw.

"Hush! He is in there." At a word from their leader the moujiks formed a circle, elbow to elbow, round the spot where "Michel," as the Russians call Bruin, was supposed to be asleep. Nico told us to keep close together; the bear would come towards us. "Let him come very near," said he, "and then aim between the eyes. If he spring, we have always the knife. Courage!"

Nico himself was very placid, having made several rapid signs of the cross. Then all at once and all together the peasants began to make the most frightful noise that I ever had heard in my life, beating the pines, giving vent to wild, incoherent cries, and shouting themselves quite hoarse. In a few minutes another sound mingled with the human ones.

"He is getting up," said Nico, grimly. Then the creature appeared. He was very big, quite enormous, in fact, and of a most lovely pale-gray color. He shook himself languidly and moved in our direction. We shouldered our rifles. "Now!" cried Nico. Serge pulled his trigger, and I did nothing. There was a cloud of smoke, and through it we could see two huge paws beating the air. Before I could fire, Nico had made a bound forward, and his bayonet disappeared, plunged into Michel's breast. With a horrible roar the beast rolled forward upon the snow. In my excitement I then fired off two shots as a sort of pean of joy, and at the risk of killing a moujik or two, after which I felt like running away. The bear was writhing in his last convulsions.

"I hit him, did I not?" asked Serge, running up.

"That is very possible, *Barin,*" replied the peasant, touching his cap; he was too deferential to take the credit to himself, although we all knew perfectly well that Serge's ball had hardly grazed him. The fact is, we had all lacked calmness and skill. Isoph went to fetch a sledge, while Nico cleansed the victim. We distributed rubles among the men, and, Nico having assured me that the bear was absolutely riddled with our balls, we gave him a handsome present. We then all had some brandy. Nobody was duped, but we had seen a bear-hunt, and spent a great deal of money.

February 22.—I found the witness I wanted in Bezdany, and he will be in Petersburg next week. Madame Krioukoff parted from me almost affectionately. "You must come back in the summer for the mushrooming," she said. "It is very amusing, and requires no fire-arms. We will get you up a fine picnic, and you will have some of our sterlet soup."

Serge told her she was an old goose, at which she laughed amiably, as much as to say, "Boys will be boys." She seemed to look upon us as mere children, and, in fact, full-grown men are childish enough, God knows!

February 25, *Petersburg.*—I have been with her nearly all the day. The children's quadrille took place on the ice at the Tauride, and there was a great turnout of all the women *à la mode*, young gallants, and the diplomatic corps. One puts on one's skates within the old palace which his royal mistress bestowed upon Potemkin, and where the favorite gave in Catharine's honor those royal entertainments which surpassed in splendor those we read of in the "Arabian Nights."

The Countess Wasia de Barythine was coquetting with Berg in the great *salon*. She had taken off her boots and was warming her tiny feet in their red hose before the fire. Berg seemed out of sorts and only half attentive. He is very cold with me. He too is touched by that more dangerous wand than any the pretty little Countess wields.

The band was playing on the shores of the desolate lake, with its gray, dim, overhanging skies, from which swoop down the low-flying birds, while in the pauses the Tziganes regaled us with songs, whose strange melodies run through all the gamut of love, of pain, and of resignation. The slide was crowded with gay cavaliers piloting their lovely burdens down on their sledges, which slipped like flashes of light and with an impetus carrying them half across to the other side of the ice-bound waters. I joined Lady Xavier, who was sitting alone disconsolately on a bench waiting for her daughter, and trying to keep warm by blowing on her fingers, while the skaters passed and repassed us, smoking their cigarettes, flirting and chatting, with red cheeks and redder noses. She spoke to me of Mrs. Acton.

"Is she as—as—er—eccentric as they say?" she asked. "I am told you know her extremely well."

"Mrs. Acton," I replied, both glad and sorry to talk of her, "is not one who can be quickly known."

"Oh!" said the English matron; "she poses for a Sphinx, does she?"

"I think she is one," I replied, laughing, "without any pose."

"Do you consider her clever?"

"Very."

"And handsome?"

"Yes."

"These Americans arrange themselves well," she said, apparently desiring to appear benignly indulgent. "They make a good effect, but the features are too small, too insignificant, and they really have no figures to speak of, none."

"Ah!" I found nothing better to reply.

The Soltikoff children and their little companions were forming into sets. Their screams of delight were wafted to us on the gusts of icy wind, and I was looking over my shoulder to see if *she* were not approaching.

"There is no doubt of it," continued Lady Xavier, as if to persuade herself of a foregone conclusion; "nowadays, to have any success, a woman must sail nearer the wind than formerly."

At this moment Miss Xavier passed us, apparently sailing very close indeed to the wind on the arm of Kalish, the dark Turkish attaché. Her mother's eyes followed her with maternal solicitude. Kalish is a favorite with the young girls. He possesses every requisite with which to fire an imagination of twenty. He is handsome, dreamy, melancholy, dissipated, and bankrupt.

"Your daughter skates well," I remarked, wishing to be amiable, and also wishing, oh, so much! that my beloved would arrive; and just then she did arrive, adorable, in rich garments. The women stared as she passed through them, while the men flocked like bees about her. With a hasty excuse I deserted my ambassadress, while Berg instantly forsook the Countess Wasia.

As I drew near her, trembling, there swept over me that faint imperceptible odor which bereaves me at once of my reason. She was charmingly gracious to me. She turned away from the others and distinguished me decidedly to-day. She gave me her hands for a moment, and I pressed and warmed them an instant in my own, and she allowed me to push her away from the people, on one of the sliding chairs, far, far away under the little bridge, where we paused amid the snowdrifts which lay in great sparkling mounds, and she listened to my words of wild devotion, her head a little bent towards me, her beautiful lips parted.

In the evening I was again beside her in the closely-curtained boudoir of the Legation, and a curious scene was acted between us, which I will record.

When I arrived, Mrs. North and her niece

were both in the room. After an exchange of commonplaces,—

"What is that ornament you wear on your watch-chain?" asked Mrs. North. "I have always intended that you should tell me. Is it a decoration, . . . or a religious medal?"

Now, the ornament in question is a tiny edelweiss formed by a cluster of small brilliants, which at parting the Princess Flavie clasped upon my chain. "It is no love-token, my friend," she said, sadly. "It is only the rivet of a faithful friendship; and may it protect you in battle, for war, they say, is in the air."

It would have been ungracious to refuse her little gift, and I accepted it lightly enough, with a word of playful badinage, pretending not to see the tear which hung upon the Princess's eyelashes, and the toy has been about me ever since, hardly remembered, and yet not all unwillingly worn, for surely I might keep it in commemoration of a happy escape from an unpleasant predicament in which my discretion played a more important part than my valor. Who knows? Perhaps the poor romantic girl's prayers are the most sincere and fervent which go up heavenward for me to-day. So I answered Mrs. North's question: "It was given me for a talisman, and I cynically keep it as a decoration."

"Ah!" said Mrs. North; "tell us all about it."

"Why, there is no story of interest attached to the thing," I answered. "One of the royal princesses gave it to me to protect me in battle. The edelweiss is, I believe, her pet flower, and is supposed to bring good luck."

Shortly after this, Mrs. North rose, saying that her husband had a severe cold, and she must herself superintend that he took certain remedies and his bath, all in good time, and she excused herself.

I was thus at last left alone with Daphne. I was sitting by a table on which stood a lamp whose glow fell upon her face, for the sofa upon which she reclined was drawn close under the light, which formed as it were a sort of rampart between us. Entirely careless of the purport of the words just spoken between Mrs. North and myself, I leaned towards her.

"And when will you keep your promise to me?" I cried, eagerly. "Is it to-morrow that I am to have the great joy of escorting you to the Hermitage?"

At the *Tavricheskom Sadou*, in the early part of the day, she had half consented to meet me some morning in the art world, and I was sick with longing, as usual, for the assurance that I should be with her again on the morrow. But she did not answer my question, only looking at me with an expression of disdain.

"I have heard Americans accused," she said, dryly, "of a lack of distinction and social grace and of the elegance and tact which charm in the *salon*. I am not sorry to find that even the courtiers of an older civilization can be deficient in good taste."

Her manner was so uncivil that I felt a flush of anger mount to my forehead. This allusion to her compatriots filled me with irritation and a vague jealousy. "If your own compatriots are so greatly our superiors," I said, with petulance, "I wonder you could ever make up your mind to leave them!"

I regretted the unworthy words as soon as uttered, but it was too late. She laughed a little harshly. "Ah!" she said, "I do not leave them for long; they want me back," and she placed her hand as she spoke on a pile of foreign letters which lay under the light beside her. "Here," she continued, "this one," lifting an envelope in her hand, —"this one says if I stay another month he will put a bullet through himself."

"Let him!" I said, savagely.

"Ah! but I cannot spare him."

"Why do you torture me so," I said. "For God's sake put an end to me or to my torments! You are unjust, ungenerous, and cruel. I do not understand you. What do you desire of me? What have I done? Wherein have I offended?"

Like a child she leaned to me suddenly, just touching the edelweiss with her fingers. Her voice grew a little faltering as if with suppressed excitement. She looked long into my eyes as if she would penetrate their secrets.

"What is it? what is it?" she said: "that

thing you wear? Was it not *vulgar?* parading your conquests before my aunt? vaunting your *gages d'amour* in my presence? and after . . . after . . . after this morning?"

"Vulgar!" I said. "Oh, my beloved! This girl is less to me than a sister. One breath of your splendor is more to me than her life or her death could ever be! Here! I will prove it;" and with a rapid gesture I rose and drew my sword from its scabbard. The edelweiss was fastened only by a slender clasp. With one sharp cut of the polished steel blade, one quick wrench, it fell at her feet, and rolled away towards the mantel-piece.

I shall never to my dying hour forget the beauty of her face at that moment. She was quite white except for two living spots of color high up in her cheeks, while her eyes seemed to dilate and to grow large and sombre, glowing like some wild thing's, some panther of the desert's. Her bosom heaved with exultant triumph, and I knew that she had been caught up for a moment into a woman's paradise; she had fathomed the depth of my passion for her, and its fire had for an instant scorched her own soul. This peculiar exaltation passed in an instant; the color faded and the lashes fell again and shaded the eyes. The palpitant breath came less quickly. The hands unclasped themselves and fell nerveless on her knees. She rose, and, walking towards the mantel-piece, raised the front of her lace skirts a little and—shall I say it?—gave a kick of considerable energy with the toe of her dainty high-heeled slipper to poor Flavie's ill-starred gift. It disappeared among the ashes. She turned to me then with such—oh, such a smile! The smile of a captious, but repentant child.

"It was an ugly little thing," she said. "A hideous little thing. It was absolutely disfiguring to your uniform. It was perfectly ridiculous. That princess must be—must be—very—very *stingy* to give you such shabby, silly presents!"

What mattered the dear foolish words which made us so near, which made her less the goddess to me than the beautiful shy creature my senses craved, my lips grew dry for, my arms longed to hold and press? But with a strength of will which I had hardly thought I possessed I conquered my impulse. Must not one quell the instincts of a savage ancestry if civilization is to count for aught? "Stingy, my beautiful one, stingy? Well, yes, perhaps; and, do you know, I am always scolding her for her extravagance?"

"*Il n'y a pas de quoi,*" she said, and then we both laughed, she a little wildly, and both until the tears stood in our eyes. It was such a relief after the intense tension. It was so sweet. We were so madly happy. Oh, Daphne, Daphne, were you not happy too? I sat near to her, and she let me hold her hands, in all honesty and seriousness, while I told her all. "I can have no further secrets from you," I said, and unfolded to her Flavie's story, only veiling names and places as was befitting a man of honor.

My head was so dizzied by the violent emotions of the evening that after I left her I walked far on the Nevsky in search of my lost calm. I craved the air. The moon was rising; it was not very cold. The church clock struck one when I reached the enclosure in which stands the statue of Catharine, "*Yekatierina.*" How lovingly Russians of all classes from the courtier to the moujik utter the magic name! I paused and looked up at her where she loomed from her base of red granite against the pallid stars. The piles of unshovelled snow threw up a queer uncertain reflection on the mantle of the lascivious queen, striding proudly over the heads of her crouching lovers,—Derjavin, Prince Dashnoff, Count Roumiantseff, Princes Potemkin, Suwarrow, Bedborodko, Belsky, Chichagoff; Counts Orloff and Chesminsky. To me this statue is a strangely unpleasant work of art; but as I leaned against the little brick railing, my thoughts were not of Catharine or of her favorites. A serpent's tooth had bitten me. Who is this man, this compatriot of hers, who threatens to kill himself if she does not return to him? What is his claim? Why will she never say "I love you!" and why will she always put off my avowals with vague answers as if in fear of the future? But, then, why this petulance, this distrust, this jealousy, if she does not care? Who can judge a woman's caprices? Am I merely this, a caprice, while I throw at her feet all the wealth of a profound adoration?

These baffling questions poisoned all the sweet memories of the evening. Bah! To fly from their torment I rapidly retraced my steps, and stopped for a moment at the club; a letter from Wilna was to await me there. Kalish, d'Aubilly, and two Chevalier Guardsmen were playing whist, smoking, and silent, only an occasional ejaculation escaping one of them across the green baize over which they were testing their luck and their genius.

On my way out my attention was drawn to a noisy group of men. They seemed to be making some attack on d'H., who I soon saw was a good deal under the effect of copious draughts from a neighboring punch-bowl. He seemed to be the target for some particular chaffing, at which great mirth was evoked. His replies were made in a protesting and fretful voice and always hailed by bursts of rather brutal merriment.

"*Allons, mon cher*," said one, bolder than the others, "Madame d'H. is charming, no doubt, but you cannot persuade us that you married her for her beauty." And then I heard the newly made bridegroom, but returned yesterday from his bridal-trip, say, rather thickly, "Believe me, my wife is supremely beautiful."

I advanced suddenly among them, and laid my hand rather heavily on his shoulder.

"Let him alone, let him alone!" cried the others.

"*Boudiet ochin viessielo!*"

"*Nietchevo*, it is only fun," said Berg; but I did not release my hold on the silly youth.

"Who are you?" he lisped. "Are you of the police? I was just explaining to these gentlemen——"

"Are you not ashamed of yourselves," I asked, angrily, of the group of thoughtless fellows, among whom I recognized some friends and many acquaintances, "to make this fool's young bride the subject of your jests?"

"If you say I am a fool, you lie," muttered d'H.

The young men suddenly seemed to feel rather ashamed of themselves, while Berg said, in a loud voice, "I was beginning to think myself they had gone about far enough."

"Perhaps I have had too much wine," muttered d'H., under his breath, and he did not struggle with me, and allowed himself to be propelled from the room.

"Young man," I said to him, once out upon the sidewalk, "be wise in time. Do not insist that others should appreciate your happiness." I could have laughed with the rest at the *bêtise* of a man's boasting of his young wife's charms to a party of unscrupulous and fiery gallants had not my disgust dampened my sense of humor; and then I gave him a little shove into the snow, and, hailing a passing çani, was whirled home.

February 26.—Before breakfast I met little Madame d'H. and her mother on my way to

16

the Anitchkoff. I looked in vain at the young woman for some marks of the tragedy which should already have touched her. The ladies were emerging from the Mala Sadovaya, and intent, they told me, upon a turquoise hunt in the Oriental shops of the Nevsky Prospect. I wished myself to look in at one of these depots of Persian and Turkish wares for a Caucasian dagger set in curious stones I had heard Mrs. Acton admire, and which I thought might be deftly concealed in a bunch of roses. I therefore walked for a few moments beside the mother and daughter. They were both bustling and busy; profuse in idle chatterings, the younger one, with her open pink nostrils and light eyes, looking for all the world like a pretty China rabbit.

"Adolph told me this morning he had met you at the club yesterday—no, it must have been to-day," she said, giggling. "He is not up yet. Do you believe it, mamma?"

"Clubs are ruining our youth," said the mother, severely, "both in morals and in manners."

"Ah yes, ah yes," answered Madame d'H., *distraite*, having spied some turquoise ornaments in the *vitrine*. "Cards and wine, particularly the wine. They take too much; it is very bad for the stomach. You, monsieur," she said, turning towards me reprovingly, "as one of the older men, should set a better example."

I stared blankly for a moment, murmuring some commonplace about being a poor creature with no gracious goddess to keep me at home, and left with a profound salutation, less to the young woman herself than to her innocence, ruse, or frivolity.

February 27.—My lady accorded me to-day, perhaps as a reward for discreet behavior, what might have been a great joy. She met me at the Hermitage; but two little incidents, one unimportant, one more serious, marred all of my hard-earned content. I was there punctually, waiting beneath the monolith of Finland granite. She floated in at the great front entrance between its splendid stooping figures (all honor to Leo von Klenze!) like some bird of rich plumage from a warmer clime seeking shelter from out the frozen day. She bade her servant care for her furs, and then, turning to me,—

"You can to-day exemplify your nation's love of tyranny," she said. "I put myself absolutely into your hands for guidance. I will follow you through this labyrinth of wonders wherever you lead me. You will not find me perverse; I promise to be docile."

I thanked her for the word which gave me a delicious sense of mastery and of care-taking over her, my *geliebte!* I began by giving her a lecture on Greek art, and she listened with that eager attention so flattering to the speaker and that no one can accord or withhold more effectually. I bade her admire the supple limbs of the draped goddess who has long held me in thrall, and told her that I had perceived from the first moment of her apparition in the drawing-rooms of the Sergievskaia a marked resemblance in her figure to that of this pet statue of mine.

"If a small bust and a large waist answer

to the rules of beauty, then indeed I must be correct, but what would the French mantua-makers say?"

"What *do* they say?"

"Oh, that I have a particular *chic*, a type of my own, which enables me to carry off my . . . defects and persuade people that I am well made. But I mean what do they say when my back is turned? I believe, however, Mr. Worth approves of me. He makes me stand about for hours while he drapes Greek gowns upon me."

"Your figure is perfect," I said, hotly. "Look at the statues of the modern French school! Take those feet and waists, distorted as were those of the grisettes who threw off their corsets and their tight shoes to pose to the artist as a Venus or a Minerva; then turn and see the tranquil ease of my lady here. There is not an angle!"

"I am very jealous of her," said Mrs. Acton, laughing; "but you must confess she looks a trifle stupid. Do I?"

So we moved on, and, oh, I was happy! I

was struck as usual with the purity of her taste, the justness of her appreciation and criticisms. When we grew tired of the *Marmor Bilder*, we amused ourselves examining the Kertch collection, with its Scythian, Siberian, and Oriental marbles. The objects found at Kief greatly interested my fair companion. Among them is that gold medal of Chernigoff's which bears the Slavonic inscription, "Lord, aid thy servant Basil!" These amulets were worn around the necks of the Russian princes and their wives, and as Saint Vladimir took the name of Basil, when baptized, this probably belonged to him. A jasper tazza in the gallery of Piotre Veliki, a plume which the Shah of Persia presented to the hero Suwarrow, who hastened to lay it at Catharine's feet, tea-services, caskets of silver, vermeil crystal and glass, Catharine's jewelled walking-sticks, a hundred objects from the Korghiz steppes,—all seemed to bewitch Mrs. Acton, and I could with difficulty tear her away from their contemplation. By and by we ascended the vast stairs which lead up to the picture-galleries.

While we wandered about we chatted, and I drew from my breast-pocket a few verses which I had translated from the Russian text for her into German. It was a pretty, musical thing, and at the first word or two I read off for her she took it into her pretty head she must then and there hear the whole. I was rather averse, I confess, to sitting down and reading my madrigal in so public a place, even though the great halls were almost deserted at this early hour; but *ce que femme veut Dieu le veut*, and in a few moments we were occupying two high-backed gilded chairs under the shadow of a great porphyry vase which adorns one of the apartments dedicated to Dutch art.

"I must hear it now," she said, like the wilful child that she is, "this very minute, every sweet little word of it."

Her docility, it seemed, had already evaporated, and, as usual, powerless to resist her, I meekly began to spell out the ill-written, somewhat jumbled lines. It was called "Unshed Tears," and was about as foolish and morbid as Slavonic melancholy can be made, with an added grain of Celtic ardor. I had almost reached its last wail when the rustle of garments made us look up, and the old Countess de Barythine and Madame Soltikoff passed up the floor. They hesitated a moment as if to stop and speak with us, but on second thoughts, exchanging rapid and somewhat significant glances, they concluded to walk on, only pausing long enough to bow. I must admit I felt like an idiot in my troubadour attitude, and a little vexed at Mrs. Acton's thoughtlessness in thus inviting criticism upon herself. In these things we are not in sympathy. If she noticed my annoyance she made no comment; she listened in silence to the poem, which I ended rather hurriedly, commended its sentiment and my talents as a translator, thanked me graciously, and, making a roll of the bit of paper, slipped it into her glove, where it lay snug and warm against the palm of her hand. We were just shaking off the slight restraint which this little episode and the possible reappearance of our acquaintances had cast upon us when a new, and this time more unexpected, occurrence served to give me food not now for vexation, but for positive pain. Certainly with Daphne one does not languish for lack of emotions.

As we were listlessly walking through a room crowded with stiff-necked ladies of the true Dutch type, with high foreheads and wide ruffs, varied by landscapes whose blue skies served as a background for very green trees and very yellow cows, our attention was simultaneously arrested by the life-size portrait of a young lad. In my poetic frenzy I had forgotten my catalogue, and left it upon one of the gilded chairs, but I had seen this striking picture before, and believed it to be one of the Stuart kings done in his boyhood by a great Dutch painter, probably Vandyke. The picture struck me then as it had struck me on former occasions, as a masterpiece. The boy, who might have been about fifteen, stood near a dark curtain, whose shadow fell upon without darkening his face, in a reposeful, graceful attitude, one hand resting upon the table.

He was dressed in a sombre velvet doublet, and in the picturesque fashion of his day. The face was full, with the slightly-rounded features and indistinct outlines of lingering childhood. The lips were dewy, and red as a woman's, yet were not devoid of a certain dignity and power. The chin, which was exquisite in its contour, was at once imperious and sensuous. It was a face which one felt might under evil influences grow animal and coarse; but at this early age it was as yet only tender and loving, and it seemed probable that it might remain charming even into manhood.

The hair, cut low and square across the brow, and hanging at either side upon the shoulders, was of a rich brown color, thick and curly. The brow itself, earnest and a little frowning, overshadowed two deep-set eyes of an indistinct blue-gray color; their dominating expression was one of sadness. One might go further and say that they had in them as they met the gaze the suggestion of a vague reproach. It was as if they were searching in the eyes that met them to detect some spark of disloyalty or faithlessness, and to reward it with a passionate contempt. The whole of the lithe, youthful, princely figure was tinged with something pathetic, with a strange melancholy and fascination. I had for a moment been so absorbed in my contemplation of its beauty that I had not looked at Mrs. Acton. When I did so, I know not why, my heart stood still. It was like the shock of some fatal presage. I had turned to say to her, "What a distinguished face!" but the words died out half uttered on my lips. Entirely oblivious of my very existence, Daphne stood with clasped hands before the picture, drinking in its minutest detail. I was struck not only by the dejected droop of her whole person, but by a look of positive terror which seemed to fix her eyes upon those of the youthful king. For fully ten minutes, to me an eternity, she remained immovable, speechless, evidently under the influence of some terrible and overpowering agitation. I touched her shoulder. "Come!" I said, with dry lips, and almost sternly.

She turned and looked at me. Her eyes were sunken; her features looked pinched. She shook off my touch and shrank away from me, cowering, looking about her as if for some way of escape.

"I wish," she said, "that the earth would swallow me!"

"What is it?" I asked, angrily. "What is this new torture you inflict upon me? What is this picture to you? What does your past hold which it recalls? Is it a dead husband, or a living lover?" The words were cruel, but jealousy makes us so.

She did not deign to reply, but, as if spell-bound, continued to look at the boy's lovely face until great tears welled up into her eyes.

"Oh, darling," I said, "have pity, forgive me, come away!"

But she shook me off. "How dare you?" she said. "What are you to me?"

I left her side and made my way to one of the windows, looking out with eyes that saw not into the square, half hidden by the troubled mist of fast-falling snow. I do not know how long I stood there. By and by I heard her light step behind me. She seemed to walk as if in a dream. A gust of icy wind from an open window about which some men were at work seemed suddenly to awaken her from her stupor. She passed her hand two or three times over her brow, as if to efface an enduring image.

"Forgive me, monsieur," she said, gently, "if I have been unkind to you. Some day I will explain all to you, and what those eyes have said to me, but to-day I cannot, I cannot."

I could not trust myself to answer her, and only offered her my arm silently. She took it and we went slowly down the corridor and then the stairs. Outside, a fine bright hurricane was blowing about. Mrs. Acton's coachman was standing on the sidewalk talking with Madame Soltikoff's footman. They were stamping their feet and tossing their arms to and fro, trying to keep warm while their mistresses lingered in the galleries.

I escorted Mrs. Acton to her sleigh, begged her to wrap up her throat, but I did not look at her, and when she faltered, "Shall I see you to-night?" I answered, "No, not to-night." She had shrunk from me as if I were a leper or some noisome thing, and I could not forget. All the way home this thought stung me into the intensest anger, but when the first rage of jealousy and of doubt was spent I fell into a mood of great dismay.

March 7.—I have kept from her for eight long, cursed days. God alone knows the misery of those wretched hours. I can exist no longer.

March 9.—Yesterday in the morning I went to her. She had sent me many summonses, but I had not heeded them. What was I in her life? Had she not asked me? I found her alone. She received me, as I thought, coldly, and all the pent-up fire that had burned within my heart surged to my lips. I think I must have found the untutored eloquence which genuine pain teaches, that cry of the heart whose sincerity is its force.

"I know," I said, "that at that moment some memory of your old life in far-off

America held you, and that you hated your present and me. But see! I was thrown away from you like a vile despised thing, and like a vile despised thing I have crawled back to your feet. Daphne, listen, I will know the truth! I have given you now every aspiration of my life, its every hope and dream. It is too late to recall them. I will follow you like a dog to the ends of the earth if you command me, throw to the winds all I have toiled for all these years, every ambition of youth, every hope of fame, or lift you to my side and proudly proclaim you my crown, my sovereign, before a world that you are made to adorn, but to-day I stand before you to know the truth from your own lips. If you have smiled upon me to fan some vain vagary born of your vanity or your idleness, given me in exchange for the best my soul can offer you, only the husks of a woman's fitful fancy, be generous, speak, while I could yet forgive you, speak while I could yet thank you for a disillusion that shall be complete enough to save us both! Do not debase me further, for to-morrow I may throw even my honor at your feet. If anything stands between us, either in your present or your past, let it be no chimera. If it be flesh and blood I shall conquer, but I can no longer fight shadows. Daphne, I am consumed with my love for you. The first time that I saw you it was the same. Lay your cool hand upon my forehead, dear. Help me, I love you!"

She had listened to me in perfect silence, but when I had finished, like a whirlwind she rushed forward to me, heedless, reckless; she threw her arms out towards me crying, "Pardon, pardon!" Then, standing close to me, she whispered three words, three words swiftly, in French. Three words! A life's history. I knew that they were true; I had read them on those pure lips for which I had so pined. But ah, when they were mine at last, imprisoned, when I drank in great draughts of their hot, delicious sweetness! It was no timid girl's shrinking kiss which met my own, but the caress of a passionate queen. There was no need of any further words. I was too intoxicated with my happiness to demand any assurances then, and she, poor child, seemed like one weary of struggling and glad to rest quietly for a moment in my arms. Before we parted she told me that the picture had reminded her of one who loved her and who had been woven into her life. She seemed to suffer so terribly at the allusion that I shrank at the sight of her pain. I know that this was weakness, but, with the moisture of her lips yet upon mine, how could I torment her? If her kiss was for farewell, God help me, for her lips after their supreme surrender made me no promises. She has, on the contrary, expressly declared that she must return at once to her own country, and that I am not to follow her until she bids me come. I am no effem inate voluptuary; I can serve for her seven years, if need be. There must be some entanglement in her life, and the moment I had left her a hundred serpents of doubt were again stinging my heart.

In the evening, knowing I should find her there, I went to the Italians. When I entered and walked to my seat she and Mrs. North were already in their *loge.* She was all in white. Berg leaned over her, keeping a jealous eye on me from behind her shoulder, and she, *insouciante,* and at the same time animated, seemingly interested in his words, yes, I actually saw her once lean back and laugh! Prince L., who sat by me, insisted on recounting the adventures in Petersburg of La Silva, who was giving us Carmen in its coarsest form; but while she warbled "*Là bas, là bas sous la montagne,*" and the old man gossiped, I was nervously clutching my opera-glass and looking up like an idiot at Mrs. Acton, to see if I could detect what was passing in her mind. She nodded to me, and I vowed to make her wait for me, and know for once what waiting means; but when the act was over I gave up all my strategy and went up to her box like her dog, which I am. She extended two gloved fingers, motioning me to a seat behind her aunt. She seemed to be coquetting with Berg, and to relegate me to a second place, and I asked myself for the hundredth time if it were indeed this woman or some other whom I had that day crushed against my breast. When I had reached the last stage of depression, she suddenly turned and gave me a radiant smile, with tender, quivering lips, and my spirit leaped up again to her with its accustomed worship. They promised to breakfast with me to-morrow, but, except superficially, we had no opportunity for any talk, and with this meagre diet I had to be content.

March 10.—Mrs. North accompanied her niece, and I asked Berg and Prince Safvet and young Madame de Barythine and her devoted Dmitri. I was more agitated at the idea that Daphne would cross my threshold than when, a young officer of twenty, a royal visit was expected at the Caserne. I passed the morning in gross violation of my promise to confer with Narishkine at the Ministry, and in absolute neglect of all my official duties, trying to bring my rooms to such a state of order as would commend them to my lady's eyes. I personally superintended Gustav's and August's disposition of the table and flowers, the bric-à-brac and furniture, sofas, chairs, cushions, and fires. I passed in review the various photographs which adorned the mantel and *étagères*, and confiscated such as might arouse a moment's uneasiness in the breast of my lovely guest.

I will say here, in parenthesis, that I might have spared myself the trouble, as she did not once glance in the direction of those which remained. Daphne, unlike other women, is never eager or curious. But is she loving? She has certainly fully fathomed the power of indifference, an indifference which seems to acknowledge and grant no claims. She leaves one absolutely free, but this magnanimity is bitter-sweet!

Among the photographs which I threw into the fire was one of Nathalie's torso which I had left upon my table, because of a certain nervous strength in the outline which had caught my fancy. She had sent it to me since her hasty flight from Russia after Strogonoff's suicide, with a newspaper clipping expatiating on her Viennese triumphs. One night after dancing the Kamarinskaia she was called out fifteen times, covered with flowers, and one of her slippers was put up at auction and sold for two thousand marks. "My cheeks were wet with tears," she wrote, "for it was poor Strogonoff who first taught me that dance, and I thought of him, of Russia, and of you, cruel man, whose horrible heartlessness has not yet killed my love. In a P. S. she adds, "They say *she* is going back to America without you." Where did the little viper get this bit of information, I wonder!

I left some family portraits and all those of the royalties; while Flavie's, with her hair in *bandeaux*, had such an air of respectability and austere virtue that I allowed it to remain upon the *étagère* over which she has presided ever since I unpacked. Poor girl! and yet how truly these women who know no arts can love us!

So Daphne came. How dear she was! and she seemed happy; and how thankful was I that my adored one should bring her loveliness to grace my poor table!

The breakfast, which had given me some

anxiety, was excellent, and the ladies' bouquets seemed to please them. The conversation was animated and everyone at ease and apparently well content. Dmitri, to be sure, was tiresome, fulfilling the assertion that "There is nothing so fatiguing as the conversation of a lover who has nothing to hope and nothing to fear." Mrs. Acton, who declares herself accomplished in chirosophy, read my hand's lines during the *déjeuner*, causing much merriment thereby. "I see," she said, "impulsive valor mingled with a certain inflexibility. It is eminently a hand of activity. You are a soldier, not a philosopher. Women will only have such influence upon your destiny as you choose to accord them. You are ambitious, master of yourself, eminently conservative, with an immense respect for authority."

Some one begged to look at her hand. "My hand," she said, "betokens love of change, an American's lamentable absence of reverence, and acute dislike of being bored."

"Does it not betoken some cruelty?" I asked, low.

"No," she replied; "pitifulness has been my bane. I am cruel only to myself."

"Are you sure of this?" I asked, laughing. "Did anybody ever bore you . . . and live?"

"It is evident," turning to her aunt, "that monsieur has not stopped in country-houses in America. People have bored me there by the hour, and I regret to say that they still survive."

"Daphne, how can you be so unpatriotic?" cried Mrs. North.

"The nice people always leave the day they are wanted, and the dull ones remain until one is ready to curse God and die."

"I don't doubt you have often treated people so, Daphne," said Mrs. North.

"Thank you, *ma tante*, for the compliment. I don't wonder you think I am one of those who stop too long."

"Don't angle for compliments. You know perfectly well you think yourself one of the nice ones who always leave too soon. But surely no one ever departed from Quimby before you desired. She is a spoilt little thing," she said, turning to me.

"Quimby is your country home, is it not?"

"Yes, and a dear place."

"Do you miss it?" She was on my left, and I could catch her words. There was a ring of self-scorn in her low tones.

"I have thought lately that if I could blot out America and all I own there, and all of my past and all of my probable future, and just live to-day, *cevodnia*, this Russian day, this Russian hour, this Russian moment, forever and forever, I should be *glad*." The last word was a sigh.

I felt myself grow pale with the nearness of her terrible loveliness. Berg sat with wide eyes, not hearing her, but gazing at her as if hypnotized. The others were still looking at each other's hand-lines. Young Madame de Barythine wished to have her hand read, and Dmitri's. She seized Mrs. Acton's across Berg, comparing it with her own.

"What is this deep line you have crossing your palm?"

"Ah, that is my safeguard, stronger to a woman than religion or morality."

"And that is——"

"The fear of disgust. Do you not think," she continued, addressing the fair Wasia, "that the fear of disgust is a rampart for us to hide behind?"

Madame de Barythine adjusted her lorgnon, but not finding this "safeguard" in her own pink palm, turned and gazed helplessly about the table. "*Elle est drôle!*" she said, under her breath, and then she turned and chided Dmitri for being so dull.

The morning waned. All I have of her now is the vague perfume which she has left behind her, and a little forgotten veil, which I have fallen upon and fairly devoured.

March 11.—My *procès* is won. The offending editor has been locked up for six months. It should have been for six years. The court is all wreathed in smiles of congratulations. Humph! The Empress has given me her picture, and lisped some friendly words to me as I bowed over her outstretched fingers.

Even the Czar's impenetrable visage lighted up with its rare smile. There is a rout at the Anitchkoff. The maids of honor are very condescending and gracious; they flutter about like little butterflies, with their knots of blue ribbon caught on their left shoulders in their diamond monograms. Daphne is not there, but the thought of her lends wings to my fancy, and I let myself be cajoled and petted, while my mind wanders off to that "gay to-morrow" in which one's mistress is never cold. I am in a good humor. When I reach home I enclose two thousand rubles in an envelope, and direct them to the far-off address in the slumbering provinces where the editor's family await the term of his punishment. They are poor.

March 12.—We seem to have drifted back, at her desire, into our old relations. I will not be importunate or indelicate. Something tells me that to press my suit too boldly now would be to jeopardize my own happiness. She will accord me no more favors, and I must perforce bow to her decree.

This afternoon she deigned to visit with me

the church of Our Lady of Kazan. I was, as usual, early at the rendezvous. On entering the church I found a marriage in progress. The singers were shouting "Let Isaiah rejoice!" in their most jubilant voices, and the great cathedral seemed to tremble in a responsive sympathy to the joyful hymns of the choristers. As I drew near to the circle of friends and the few stragglers whom the ceremony had attracted, the bride and groom were just moistening their lips at the cup which is termed the cup of bitterness. I watched them as they walked three times round the altar, while the pages followed them with painstaking outstretched arms, holding over their heads the golden crowns. The bride's taper seemed in dangerous proximity to her veil. She had a funny little pug nose, was blonde, commonplace, and composed, while the groom, a mere boy, looked frightened to death. They then prostrated themselves before the Virgin of the Iconostase, while I wandered away a little, wondering why Mrs. Acton did not arrive.

When the wedding-guests had dispersed, I returned to this ancient Virgin, hoping her serenity might quiet my impatience. She was brought from Kazan in 1579, and is incrusted with fabulously valuable jewels, among them that great sapphire presented to her by the Grand Duchess Catharine Paulovna, and a huge diamond which was floated down the Volga by Ivan Vassilievitch to Moscow, and thence to Petersburg by Peter the Great. The verger seemed to disapprove of my long contemplation, and jostled me as he passed, and I moved on to examine the military trophies which make of this church a species of arsenal. I paused a moment by the tomb of General Prince Smolenskoi, who prayed upon this spot before going to battle, and it was here that Mrs. Acton found me.

"True to your martial predilections," she said. We walked about the church together, speaking little, but upon me was that sense of ecstasy which her presence ever brings. By and by we sat down side by side under a swinging lamp and watched a bent old woman mumbling her prayers. At last we came out under the colonnade and paced up and down, waiting for the Norths' equipage, which was to be sent back for Mrs. Acton from the Xaviers' reception, whither her aunt had gone. Mrs. Acton spoke of the hope and consolation the Russian seems to find in his religion. "After all," she said, "old age has nothing else. What shall I do when I am old? Mine is such a fitful faith."

I interrupted her, beginning to speak of the pleasures of age and its compensations. She lifted her hand and made a motion as if to lay it across my lips.

"I know all you would say. In your family you have a beloved, gentle-souled old lady, or an uncle of ninety who has kept his front teeth, and you yourself anticipate, nay, feel sure, that the end of your life shall be dignified and serene. No doubt, no doubt we can all find among the wrecks of life a few instances of arrested decay, where the body—and even the heart—have been tenderly dealt with by fate, but oh, *mon ami!* old age at the best is hideous, and how futile and superficial is the intercourse of the young and of the old. How restive they make us! Have you ever knelt at some veteran's feet and asked him almost with agony to show you the way? Have you craved to open yourself to him in confidence, longing for his guidance? I will wager that the answer was either impatient rebuke or cowardly evasion. The mind grows lazy, the heart torpid. I think the passions have no memory when they do not crystallize into malice. Older people have harassed me with censure, with ill-timed, foolish counsels, have quarrelled with, fretted at, and well-nigh distracted me; but where is the calm, just spirit which, looking back on the battle and its dust, on its humbling defeats and hardly-won triumphs, praises, pities, encourages, saying, 'Thus and thus was it with me; take heart, child!' No; depend upon it, monsieur, old people are horribly frivolous, busy with petty and soul-debasing trifles, and that is why I pity them so profoundly.—Have you ever been very angry?"

she asked me suddenly, as if following some train of recollection.

"Yes, very."

"When?"

"Last night, with Berg, when he looked at you as he did."

"And how was that?"

"Abominably, and you do not resent it."

"What folly! I do not even see the man."

"Well, I do, and I grow murderous."

"Nonsense! I don't believe you. I mean very, very, very angry?"

"Have you been so?"

"Yes."

"Tell me about it."

"Ah, there too were older people who should have helped me! I had sacrificed my life, my youth, and then . . . they failed me, . . . they would not understand." She spoke with suppressed feeling, as if at the memory of some deeply-resented wrong.

"And you were angry?"

"Don't let me talk of it," she said, hurriedly; "mine is not a forgiving nature."

As she spoke, she stepped quickly out from under the arcade into the square, whither I followed her, and we were startled to find that it was almost night. I peered about in vain, for the sleigh and Alexei were nowhere to be seen. My own equipage was being walked hither and thither, up and across the Nevsky, where the usual crowd were promenading with concealed faces, unreal and shadowy. The statues of Smolenskoi and Barclay de Tolly stood out against the dying day on an horizon gemmed with stars.

"How very strange!" Mrs. Acton shivered slightly, coming out from the shelter into the cold. With me she leaves always a warmth and light, and I feel neither cold nor darkness by her side. I offered her my sleigh, but I saw her hesitate.

"It is so well known, so conspicuous," she said, a little nervously.

"You cannot stand here any longer," I said, authoritatively, and hailed a miserable drosky, dismissing my own conveyance. I motioned to my servant to jump on the box, and had soon ensconced Mrs. Acton in a corner of the wretched vehicle, and myself by her side.

It is not customary in Petersburg for a young woman to drive alone through the streets at dusk with any man, much less with one who must, by this time, be well known in her world as an ardent admirer. I felt vexed for her, and could see that she was herself annoyed. The perfect composure, however, the die once cast, with which she accepted the irremediable, and her avoidance of the subject during our homeward drive, struck me as distinctly high-bred. My proud darling!

Light women explain, flush, play the prude, at the "*Qu'en dira-t-on?*" Daphne is sure of herself. She never explains anything, and allows others to form their own conclusions. This haughtiness is dear to me, with its assurance of an innate purity. As she arranged her draperies I felt as if she were encased in armor.

The young woman was safe from any whisper of mine, even in praise of her grace and her beauty, nor would I have dared remind her that her lips had once for one moment been mine. How we stout-hearted warriors quail before a woman's possible displeasure! During our homeward drive we exchanged few words, and these remained within the bounds of the most absolute reserve. Why is it that the very first time I saw this lady I felt as does the swimmer when he passes from the shallow into the ocean waters? They look like the others; they are still, quiet, and alluring, but he knows that he has slipped into the deeps. He hears the light sigh of the beginnings of life; nameless creatures press around him, whose shapes are unfamiliar, and he shivers, for he knows he has entered into the untried seas.

March 13.—I wonder if what she says of me is true: that I am too conservative? Have I already in me the germs of that narrowness which she so deprecates in the old? She once said that perfectly-satisfied people could never be reformers. She was right.

March 14.—Reading one of Dostoievsky's dolorous stories. How different from the labored grossness of the French writers of to-day is the realism of these Russians! It has kept in touch with the heartaches of the world, and has a sympathy which the French have lost. One never hears the *ricanement* of its unbelief. There is still left a breath of the illimitable. I read a little from the original. This boneless, supple tongue charms me, although I am stupid at grasping its intricacies. And what a queer people, with their intense patriarchal institutions, taking refuge under the wings of an absolute throne! "*Pourri avant d'être mûre!*" We shall see. I fell to singing the words of Tutchef:

"Comme le globe terrestre
Est enveloppé de l'océan,
Ainsi la vie terrestre
Est entourée de songes."

Is my passion, too, a dream?

March 15.—We court-fossils are accustomed to breathe only evil smells or perfumes. These Americans seem to bring us fresher air. How it woos the enfeebled lungs! Air! air! Near her I feel the dust of my old prejudices blow away. She told me to-day, suddenly, that she must return to America. I try in vain to combat her resolve. My pleadings seemed only to agitate her, and my prayers were useless.

March 17.—Mrs. North, in her bizarre, rapid way, said to me this evening, "I wish Daphne to accompany me to the Riviera, where I am going while Mr. North runs over to America for a few weeks to look after his private affairs, but she insists that she must return with her uncle, and grows excited if I urge her to remain. In fact, she seems in feverish haste to start. I don't pretend to understand her, and I doubt if anybody ever will, unless, indeed, monsieur," she added, smiling, "you have fathomed her. I wish we might yet persuade her to remain among us. I confess I have thought her very happy here. I am afraid," she continued, lowering her voice, "that she is contemplating something self-sacrificing and uncomfortable, and her sacrifices are apt to be tremendous."

I am profoundly distressed. I now feel sure

that she hides some entanglement from me, and I also feel sure that it is nothing which in any way casts discredit upon herself. I will trust to the nobility of her nature and place all my hope in the future. In a few weeks, at best, I can follow her and know my fate. I cannot persecute her now. She seems unhappy.

March 28.—She is gone!

Leaning on her uncle's arm, in her dark-red coat with its black furs, she entered the *gare*. A large party had come to see her off. I stood in the shadow. She carried my flowers in her hands and a knot of them at her throat. She looked pale under her little toque and black veil. Her eyes sought me. I stepped forward quickly to her side into the garish light. People who were hurrying hither and thither stopped and stared at our party, for we formed a group in striking contrast to the rest of the waiting crowd, the women in light dinner dresses only half concealed by their dark wraps, and the men in full evening toggery. She leaves them all; she draws away her hand from her uncle's arm and places it in mine. The others fall back, seeming to understand, and gather about Mrs. North, who is also leaving for the south. Mr. North accompanies his niece to America. The First Secretary of Legation, who is to be *chargé* during the Minister's short absence, is piloting Mrs. North, and maids and men servants come after, laden with bags and furs.

Enigmatical to the last, Mrs. Acton peremptorily forbids me to follow her immediately. "I must go back to my own country," she says, hurriedly. "Until then I can say nothing. I will write you at once. I will write, I promise. Ask me no further questions, but remember you are free."

"No," I answer; "I am not free, for I love you!" and when I say these words she listens, —listens with avidity, with parted lips and dreamful eyes. What means this, if not the token of an answering love?

The whistle blows. A railroad official asks me rather roughly if I want seats, and requests our party not to block the way of travellers; then recognizes and salutes me, muttering a hasty apology. An old Russian woman carrying a big bundle pushes up against us. I can almost feel Daphne's heart beat against mine. We all step out upon the platform. I grasp Mrs. North's hand in farewell. Hers is cordial, almost affectionate. Then I hold Daphne's a moment, whispering in her ear, "I love you until death!" There are two crimson spots upon her cheeks now, but she is dry-eyed. She enters the car. The train moves off. I can see her face but dimly through the frosty pane. The others wave hats and handkerchiefs; some of the women are a little tearful. "*Dobravo putie!*" they cry. Berg is funereal. They all go away and leave me. I mechanically raise my cap. The train has moved out—I am alone.

April 2.—I went this evening to the Isaacquientski Sabor. The Chantres de la Cour were singing for some special service. Montferrand is a clever artist. How simple and imposing is this edifice! Built on a marsh, how securely it seems to stand! Will it one day crumble like our most solid hopes? I gazed curiously up into the prestol with its steps of porphyry, its dome of malachite, and its walls of lapis-lazuli. It makes the eyes blink. I sat in a dark corner and listened to the quaint, sad strains of the boy choristers. The one word "*gospode*" rose up faintly and far into the dome. All the others were indistinct. It sounded more like a plaint than an invocation. I knelt a moment; I could not pray, but I gazed up at the pale ardent Christ of the great window, and his eyes seemed to meet mine, full of a human anguish. Later I went up to the dome. I had not made the ascent before. When, a little breathless, I reached the top, looking northward, I could see, across the river, Basil's Island, and Aptekarski, and the Gelagin, where the people go on summer nights. The desolate fortress, in bitter irony, looked like some enchanted palace, and the Dvortsovy and Troitskoi bridges, like sharp, dark furrows upon a waste of snows.

The great height calmed me. My eyes seemed to pierce the mists far, far, I even fancied to where the Atlantic tosses its angry, cruel waters. *Ce lointain sans forme qui appelle à lui.* She is indeed gone.

April 11.—I walk almost daily in the *Lietnê Sadou.* At first the guards, with the acumen of their class, looked encouragement at me, as if to say, "She is late, but will yet come." Now, after the salute, they do not notice me. To-day they winked at each other, as if to say, "She will come no more." One day I must have slept from cold on one of the benches. I awoke with a sweet, wild tumult in my poor old heart. I thought I had seen her shadow fall across my feet. I rose and shook myself, and stumbled blindly out into the deserted alleys. I like this garden very much, although it plays me such tricks. Of how much torture is the human brain capable? Men have always said I was very sane. I do not know. Let me see? Fifteen—eighteen days,—we will say twenty. Surely, surely the letter will come soon. She said, "I will not write until I reach New York." Twenty days is enormous. It permits the ship to break a shaft, and the train to be blocked for forty-eight hours, and—fool that I am!

April 27.—One more day. If the letter be not here to-morrow, I leave for America. What is this woman, to play so on my heart-strings? . I hate her!

April 28.—I went to see old Madame de Barythine. She received me in her faded *salon*, with its fine hangings and pictures. There are three portraits of herself when she was young. She does not affect the worn-out liveries of youth, but has the good taste and the courage to dress as befits her age, and to be gray-haired. A rather shabby young man served tea in little golden cups. She found fault with him for not being dressed, and confided to me once more that since the depression of the ruble and the enormous expenditure of her husband's mausoleum she had sent to her estates for young moujiks and tried to train them as house-servants. "But," she added, "they are a lazy, dirty lot, and I am entirely discouraged." Her relatives tell me she is very rich.

Bent on entertaining me, she showed me numerous photographs of the late Count, and also one of the Princesse X., who she said was his first love. "My husband," she said, "had two loves in his life, the Princesse and myself. He married me after this liaison was over. It nearly broke her heart. He was a fascinating man. She had two sons. They are very nice fellows. My husband always assured me that they were not his—let us hope so. Would it amuse you to see my jewels?"

I followed her into a smaller drawing-room fitted with bookcases surmounted by mirrors. She produced a small key from her watch-chain, and, unlocking a drawer, pulled it open, and, taking up a tray, quite dazzled me. She scooped up and dangled before me such magnificent black pearls, such rivers of diamonds and of rubies. There were turquoises, too, that looked like robin's eggs. She enjoyed fondling them with her fat white hands. "My nieces wish me to make the disposition," she said, "but there is really no hurry. I promise nothing. They may all yet go to deck the icons of our parish church. *Entre nous, cher Comte*, my nieces are heartless enough hussies, not worth much. Ida would not cross the street to give a pleasure to her old aunt, and Wasia,—well, Wasia is charming enough, but . . . you know what they say. By the way, how do you live on without your lovely American?" And the old lady looked up at me with keen, kind eyes.

"I am not alive at all."

"Ah! I knew, I knew!"

She was very tactful, and spoke in praise of my beloved. She poured balm into my wounds, purring over me as women like to do, and I sat with a sense of comfort and content by her fireside, sipping her tea and listening to her soft garrulity.

"Eh! Why not, why not? She is free, she is rich; it would be excellent, perfect. They are very pretty, these Americans, and clever too, I imagine; a little accentuated, perhaps, but what will you have, my dear? The world must move on and one must march with it. My *Figaro* tells me in their large cities they have quite a society. It is wonderful! *Qu'en dirait* Bismarck? Eh!" And she chuckled.

And I, who hate visits and ugly old women, sat on, dreading to move out into the outside wilderness of the world.

April 30.—When Gustav opened my shutters this morning I had a sense of impending doom. My porter came up with that *triste*, confused, and irresolute manner which characterizes nearly all of these sons of the pallid steppes, and is in such quaint contrast with the robustness of their appearance, a look as if they were in contemplation of something puzzling and elusive. He came to tell me that the mail-train had met with an accident and was delayed at Eydtkuhnen, and that the papers and letters would not be delivered until noon. A messenger from the Embassy had stopped to bring me these tidings. He went off humming a Slav ditty, the folk-lore of the fishermen on the great rivers and of the Cossacks of the Ukraine, which he doubtless learned in childhood in his village of the Don. These songs are full of a burning tenderness and melancholy, and seem to rest with sorrow upon one's heart. Perhaps it was this song, indistinctly heard, which had caused me to awaken with a peculiar expectation.

When the courier did at last arrive I knew that my hour had come. I did not open my letter then; it burned me. I hurried into my coat and cap and got out into the street. I was hardly conscious of whither I went until the old guards of the *Lietnê Sadou* saluted me. I had, indeed, crossed the square and the bridge like a somnambulist. The air was soft and heavy. There was that lurid light in the dull sky which in summer presages thunder. To-day I knew it was only the vapors caused by a sudden thaw. I could hear the distant rumbling of the cracking ice on the Neva; the pulsation of its imprisoned waters came to me, half stifled, like the sigh of a hidden and distrustful life. Soon the river would be breaking up; soon the great ice-blocks would come floating down from Lake Ladoga.

I found my way to a seat where we had often rested together, near the Czar's tea-house. It was in a quiet alley under the dripping trees, one of our favorite spots. I sat down, and, with fingers which trembled, I opened my great coat, unfastened the breast of my uniform, and drew forth the letter. But I still hesitated to break the seal. No, not yet, not yet! I turned it over and over. I looked at the post-marks and the address. I gloated over it as a miser over his ducats. I had suffered so much! Here, where I had loved her so wildly, where she had leaned so near to me, I should at last read my fate. The place was meet enough. In-doors I should have stifled with the tumult of my emotion.

A sparrow came flying from a neighboring tree and tumbled about in the mud close to my feet. It seemed very tame. I suppose it, too, had its desires, was looking for its crumbs. I almost wished the letter might be short. I have faced bullets calmly, but this letter unnerved me. I had a foolish feeling that I might be struck with blindness before I could finish it. I only wanted the one word, "Come!" But when I had opened it I saw that it was of several pages. This is what I read:

"Do not curse me—this is all I implore! Oh, noblest, best, truest, bravest of men! when you open this letter I shall be married to another. Listen! You know my first marriage. It was nothing. He loved me. I sacrificed myself for my family. He thought that he was going to die at once and leave me all and his name. I cannot go over it now. You know enough. Well, all those years, those years of widowed youth, when I was estranged from my family and went home to my splendid loneliness, poor, unhappy child that I was, there was one who had a care for me. Oh, how he loved and succored me! He is not a hero, like you, but he loved me. He is not beautiful as a god, like you, but he loved me. Such a love! So deep, so true, so tender, so strong, so simple. He watched over me all those years. I met him—no matter where—in the world, I think. He stood over and over again between me and calumny. When I was reconciled to my people, it was through his advice and aid. At last it came to be that all my pleasures were the result of his sacrifices; all of my peace was at the expense of his. When I was free, he wanted me, and I pledged myself unhesitatingly to him. But . . . I could not then. I told him to wait: he waited. I said, 'Let me go to my uncle in Russia; do not follow me; there my term of mourning will expire, and I will return and all shall be as you desire.' I wanted time; I had stood too close to death.

"The first time I ever saw you I was dazzled by your power. I have mumbled for years 'Lead us not into temptation' upon my knees, but in Russia I really prayed for the first time. I almost hated you! Do you remember the day we passed the club, and again when you read those verses to me at the Hermitage? I did it expressly. I wished to disgust and repel you, and I did both, for a moment, I believe, but not for long enough, and I was weak, and we were weak, were we not... dear? But nothing that I could have done would have repelled or disgusted *him*, even for a moment. I could never have suited you. Berg, too, tried to harm you in my estimation. He told me that you had a liaison with a woman called Nathalie; that all your world knew of it. I did not believe him, and yet I found myself strangely jealous, for I know that you are charming to women. I should have been madly jealous of you; it would have debased and killed me. Well, it was no use. When I left I knew not what I should do. After the evening that I let you love me my self-respect was gone. I was, oh, how miserable! I felt worse than the lowest fallen. Oh, I suffered! You see, I love beautiful things too much: the life over there, the moonlit nights, the *troïkas* flashing over the ice, your brilliant talk, your courtly homage, your splendid love! Now I must never again think of them.

"I reached the port and he came. I saw him standing on the ugly black dock of our great American town in the cold light of the damp dawn. He had stood there half the night, waiting. I shall never forget his eyes as they first looked into mine. The sword of his sufferings pierced my heart. My letters had been cold and then had ceased. He knew nothing. He grasped my hand, and his first words were, 'Had I not had perfect faith in your purity and in your loyalty I should have sent a bullet through my brain long since.' I noticed how loosely his clothes hung upon him, and a peculiar thinness about his throat and cheeks which are naturally full with the roundness of health and of youth. He had not complained; he is not dramatic. Do you remember the picture in the Hermitage gallery? It had his mouth and his eyes, and I knew then that if I broke with him for you they would forever look into mine and haunt me with an endless remorse. You had crossed my path for an hour, but he was all bound up with a tragic past. Yet I faltered! but that is over. My friend, good-by. I shall never look back for an hour. I once kissed your lips—do you remember it? How could God make such treachery so sweet! I now press my own to your forehead like a dying sister, and I pray that the angels whom I have so offended may give you of their peace. My friend, farewell."

For a moment after the perusal of this letter I sat like one stricken with palsy, stupidly looking at the little bird that was hopping about again pecking at the soiled snow, watching me furtively with its round silly eyes. Then a sudden fury and despair seized me, and I tore the letter with my teeth. I crushed and mangled it as if it had been the soft fingers which had dealt the cruel blow, and in so doing I was conscious of a certain relief and pleasure. The perfume of her hands seemed to linger on the paper, and shook my senses with memories of poignant sweetness. A cold sweat broke over my forehead. I gathered up the torn bits and threw them from me, crushing them under my heel and spur into the snow. They were soon an unrecognizable mass of filthy pulp. One white piece, indeed, fluttered away, and the bird picked it up, eying me still timidly, and flew off with it to build its nest. I remember I thought, "What a mockery!"

I have no recollection of how long I sat in the garden, how many minutes or hours I paced its narrow walks, in frenzied haste, each breath that I drew hurting me like a knife. I only know that my youth died. When the rage had spent itself, at last, I came back and threw myself on the seat exhausted, and then I pulled my cap down over my eyes and wept, wept as women do at a child's disgrace or a lover's betrayal. God grant that I may never see her face again!

THE END.

PRINTED BY J. B. LIPPINCOTT COMPANY, PHILADELPHIA.

www.ingramcontent.com/pod-product-compliance
Lightning Source LLC
LaVergne TN
LVHW010557110826
845149LV00003B/680

9781418187552